A PINCH OF HOMICIDE

KATHLEEN SUZETTE

Copyright © 2024 by Kathleen Suzette. All rights reserved. This book is a work of fiction. All names, characters, places and incidents are either products of the author's imagination, or used fictitiously. Any resemblance to actual events, locales or persons, living or dead, is entirely coincidental. All rights reserved. No part of this book may be reproduced or transmitted in any form or by any means, electronically or mechanical, without permission in writing from the author or publisher.

❦ Created with Vellum

SIGN UP

Sign up to receive my newsletter for updates on new releases and sales:

https://www.subscribepage.com/kathleen-suzette

Follow me on Facebook:

https://www.facebook.com/Kathleen-Suzette-Kate-Bell-authors-759206390932120

CHAPTER 1

"Just look at that beautiful sky," my best friend, Lucy Gray said.

I nodded, glancing up at the brilliant blue sky. The sun was shining, and birds were singing. Ever since Lucy and I had hit the running trail this morning, I had been smiling from ear to ear. March had blown in all blustery and full of rage with its snow and windstorms, and we had stayed indoors as much as we could. But we were nearing the end of April now, and we'd had three sunny days in a row. I knew better than to jinx things by mentioning it, but I couldn't help myself. "I know, three whole days of sunshine. I can hardly believe it."

She glanced sideways at me. "We weren't going to talk about it out in the open."

I chuckled as we continued running. "I know, I'm sorry." Early April had been just as blustery as March, so these three days in a row meant a lot to us. Summer would be here before we knew it, but it still wouldn't be soon enough.

She nodded. "I'm afraid to look at the weather forecast for the rest of the week. If it says snow, I'll cry."

"Me too." When you live in a state like Maine, and you're close to the end of the snowy season but not close enough, it can be tough. I was more than ready for the snow to be gone and for the warmth of the late spring sunshine. Because it would be late spring before we got much sun.

"I'm ready for lazy days on the beach with a good book," she huffed out as we ran.

It could be said that we were actually just moving at a slow jog. We had been running on treadmills during the winter to avoid the biting cold, and the road always felt different once we got outside again. It would take a few days for us to make the adjustment, so I was hoping for more warm weather to help the process.

"I hear you. I'm ready too." There was a lone figure up ahead running toward us. "I wonder who that is?" The woman wore a pink knit hat on her head and was dressed in pink and white running clothes.

Lucy squinted and sidestepped a small puddle. "I don't know; we're not close enough to tell."

We ran on, enjoying the warm sun, and when we got closer to the solitary figure, I realized it was Laura Landers, a woman we knew from around town. I tucked an errant lock of my long red hair back beneath my knit hat.

Laura smiled when we got closer and waved at us. "Hello, girls! Are you enjoying the beautiful weather?"

We both nodded and came to a stop in front of her. "Yes. Isn't it beautiful?" I asked. "I'm so excited that we can run outside again. I just hope we get a few more beautiful days like this."

"Yeah, we don't want to jinx it, though," Lucy said, shooting me a look.

Laura laughed. "I know what you mean. I'd so rather be out in the beautiful weather than go to the gym." She rolled her eyes. "I detest the gym, but if it's all I can get, I'll take it." She laughed again. "How have you ladies been? Tell me all the news. What have you been up to? Anything exciting?"

Laura was one of those women who always brought a smile to my face. She was in her late thirties, always smiling, and never had a hair out of place. I could have resented her for that, but she was just too nice to resent for anything.

"Oh, you know how it is. We've just been waiting

out the winter for some beautiful weather so we could climb out of our dreary holes and get some sunshine," I said. "How about you, Laura? What have you been up to?"

"I've been doing the same," she said. "Holed up at home just counting the days until the weather broke."

"I know what you mean," Lucy chuckled. "But I'm the one who lives in a hole of a home; Allie lives in a mansion."

Laura laughed again. "I know. I've driven by her house. I am so envious, Allie. Your home is beautiful."

I smiled. My husband Alec and I had bought an old, dilapidated house that had been referred to as a mansion in the past, but that was an exaggeration. It was a large house. With a ballroom. Okay, maybe it was a small mansion. Alec and I had done a lot of work on the place, and I was rather proud of what we had done with it. "Mansion is an exaggeration. But what about you, Laura? What are you up to?"

"Oh gosh, my son Jacob is away at college for his first year, and that gives me all the time in the world to do whatever I want, but I still never have enough time to do everything I want," she laughed. "Right now I've got a clothing drive to help put on. I'm helping my sister-in-law at one of the big churches in Bangor this afternoon, and next week I'll be helping out at the homeless shelter there. It seems like I am always on the go." She grinned.

I nodded. "It sure sounds like it."

"You're always helping people out," Lucy said. "I wish I could be more like you, Laura. But I'm afraid I've given in to lazing around in front of the fireplace and sipping cocoa."

She waved the thought away. "Oh, Lucy, I know you help out with things here in Sandy Harbor whenever you can. And let me tell you, it's very much appreciated. Both of you do a lot around here, and we're all thankful for that."

I smiled. "Well, we do try to help when we can. We probably should do more, but it really sounds like your plate is full."

She nodded and glanced at her watch. "Yeah, it is. But I still try to make time for fun things like running, and I've got a book club meeting this evening. And speaking of book club, I'd better get going because I still haven't finished the book we're all reading." She laughed. "Can you imagine the president of the book club hasn't done her homework?"

"Book club? Where do you have your book club?" I asked.

"It's in the meeting room at the county library. You two should join us. We meet on the third Tuesday of the month. We've got a nice little group that gets together to discuss the book we're reading. Everybody brings something to eat to share with everyone else, and we just hang out for a couple of hours, talk about the book, and then we visit for a while and eat. Those are three of my favorite things, you know. Books, talking, and eating." She laughed and tucked a lock of blonde hair that was poking out from beneath her hat back behind her ear.

Lucy and I looked at each other wide-eyed, and then I turned back to her. "We would love to come to your book club. That sounds like so much fun."

"I love nothing more than reading good books and eating," Lucy said, nodding. "What time?"

"Seven o'clock. The library closes at six on Tuesdays, but one of the librarians is a member of the book club, and she'll let you in if you just knock on the door. Janet Dixon." She made a face. "She's sort of grumpy, but she makes a mean spinach dip."

"What book are you reading this month?" I asked. I was excited about the possibility of getting together with a group of other book lovers.

"*'The Sun Grieves'* by local author Lloyd Walker. It's kind of a depressing book, but you don't need to read it; you won't have time to get it finished by this evening," she said.

I nodded. "I bet if we read fast, we'll get it done, right Lucy?"

Lucy nodded. "Oh sure, we can run down to the library after we get done with our run and check out a copy. Oh, do you think there are any copies left? If everybody in the book club is reading it, there might not be any left."

"I heard Lloyd donated a bunch of copies to the library." She rolled her eyes. "I guess he thought everybody in town would want to check it out."

I chuckled. "Well, it is kind of exciting that somebody local wrote and published a book. Maybe we'll stop by and pick up a copy. What do you all usually bring to eat for after the book discussion?"

"Anything you want. Most of us stick with sweet things, like muffins or cupcakes. But savory snacks are also good. I'm bringing chips and dip myself."

"We can whip up something this afternoon," I said, getting excited about the book club.

She nodded. "Well, don't feel you have to finish the book, but we would love to have you come by this evening. You'll get a feel for how we run the meeting, and you'll get to meet everybody there. There are usually about a dozen of us, sometimes more, sometimes less."

"I can hardly wait," Lucy said. "We'll be sure to bring a tasty snack."

She nodded. "You don't have to bring a lot. There

will be enough there that no one will be left out, and there will be coffee and hot tea."

I grinned. "I'm excited about this. I'm glad we ran into you, Laura."

She nodded. "I'm glad I ran into the two of you, too. Now then, I had better get going. I've got so much to do, and like I said, there's that book that needs finishing. I'll see you both this evening."

"We'll see you then," I said, and we continued with our run.

"This will be so much fun," Lucy said.

I nodded. "Won't it though? Now I've got to come up with something to make."

"I have to come up with something, too."

I shook my head. "She said that we don't have to bring a lot of food. If you help me with whatever we decide on, then we'll just tell them it's from both of us."

"Alright then, what ideas do you have?"

I shook my head. "I don't know, but I'll come up with something."

I hadn't been to a book club in ages, and I was looking forward to this.

CHAPTER 2

*A*fter completing our run, we opted to bypass our usual stop at our favorite coffee shop, The Cup and Bean and proceeded directly to the library to see if we could check out the book the book club was discussing this month.

We stepped into the library and the smell of old books came to me.

"Where do you suppose it is?" Lucy asked, glancing around the nearly empty library.

"They did away with the card catalog, so we'll have to look it up on the computer." I headed over to a small kiosk with a computer. It had been ages since I had checked a book out of the library. "I miss the old card catalogs, don't you?" I asked as I moved the mouse, waking up the computer.

"I do. And I miss library cards inside the front cover of each book. I don't know where the time has gone, but I bet those were removed years ago."

"It's not the same," I said as I typed in the book's title along with the author's name.

"Uh-oh. It looks like there's only one copy left." I glanced at her. "What will we do? We only have today to finish it."

She shrugged. "You've got treats to make; I can read the book aloud."

"Excellent idea. Come on, let's go find it." I headed over to the rack where I knew we would find the book. Running my fingers along the spines of the books on the shelf, they came to a stop at a green one with black print. "Here we are." I pulled the book out and showed it to Lucy.

"Oh, that's a nice cover," she squinted. "Looks like a dogwood bush."

I nodded. "Sure does. I wonder if there might be another copy hidden in the wrong place." I continued running my finger along the spines, but it looked like all the books were in their proper order, and there wasn't going to be an extra copy of the book. Giving up, I said, "I guess not."

She shrugged. "It doesn't matter. We probably won't get through the entire book anyway, and like I said, I'll just read it aloud while you cook."

I nodded. I knew better than to think that Janet Dixon would allow the bookshelves to get messy or for books to be out of order. We headed up to the front desk where she sat.

Janet looked up at us and pushed her glasses back up on her nose. "Good morning, ladies. Did you find what you were looking for?" She stood up, and with mincing steps, came to the front desk.

I nodded. "I think so. Janet, you don't happen to have any more copies of this book, do you?" I asked, holding it up. "We're reading it for a book club, and we could really use a second copy."

She narrowed her eyes at me. "Book club? This book?" She pointed at the book.

I nodded. "Yes, we're getting a late start, but this is the book they're reading."

She sighed and took the book out of my hands and turned the front cover to face us. "This is a wonderful book. You're going to enjoy it so much. I'm in the book club that meets here at the library. Are you talking about that one?"

"Yes, that's the one," Lucy said. "We're joining tonight."

"I didn't know the two of you were joining our book club. I've never seen you there before." She set the book on the counter and picked up a scanner gun to scan the inside label.

"We ran into Laura Landers this morning, and she invited us to join," I explained. "We're excited about it."

She pursed her lips and glanced at us. Her forehead furrowed. "Laura Landers," she said, as if just mentioning the name was repulsive. "Yes, I suppose she is running the book club, but that's only because she cheated to get that position."

I was surprised to hear her say this. Laura didn't seem like the kind of person who would cheat at anything, but maybe I didn't know her well enough. "Oh?"

She nodded and closed the book cover, sliding it across the counter to me. "Yes, you know how she is. Her and her friend... Adriana Bartle. The two of them couldn't pick out a decent book to read if their lives depended on it. All they want to read are those trashy romances and Hollywood gossip books. But the two of them conspired together to get the other members to vote for her, and that's how she ended up being the president of the book club. But you just wait. Cheaters never prosper. Just because she's the president this year doesn't mean she will be president again next year." She gave me a smug look as if she knew something I didn't.

I nodded slowly, not really sure what to say to all

of this. I hadn't even known there was a book club before this morning, so I had no idea what was going on between her and Laura or the other members. "That's nice that they take a vote every year."

"Yes, it makes it more fair for everyone, doesn't it?" Lucy said. She glanced at me.

Janet nodded. "That's right. It makes it fair for everyone. We have a rule that a president can't be president for more than one year. After they've served, they have to take the next two years off so that other people can have a chance at it. Otherwise, I'm sure Laura would hog the position for many years in a row." She shook her head and made a tsk-tsk sound. "Honestly, I'm surprised the other members put up with her shenanigans. Who wants to read a trashy book when they could read fine literature like this?" She tapped the cover of the book with her finger. "I know the author, Lloyd Walker, and he is such a wonderful person. His writing is exquisite, and I can hardly wait for his next book. He's working on a new one now. It's going to be published early next year. He told me he would see what he could do about getting me an advance copy. Can you believe it? I'm so excited." Her face lit up as she spoke about this new book.

"I've heard of Lloyd, and I think I've even met

him," I said. "Didn't he used to work as a high school English teacher?"

She nodded. "Yes, he said that many writers pay their dues by being English teachers before getting their big break." She chuckled. "Can you imagine? We have a famous author living right here in our town. He's such a nice man. Very open to talking about his writing process."

I smiled. I wasn't sure Lloyd Walker was famous yet, but you never knew where something might lead. "It is exciting. I'm sure he will have a wonderful career as an author. Does he still work at the high school?"

She nodded. "Yes, he's still at the high school." She sighed. "If you ask me, he's not happy there. He expects to quit after he gets the advance on his next book. Then he'll be able to spend all his time writing and will be able to publish more frequently. That's his dream. I know because he told me."

"It sounds so exciting," Lucy said. "Imagine being able to spend your days dreaming and making up characters and things for them to do. That would be so much fun."

Janet nodded. Her short red hair had faded with age, and she had a rhinestone clip on the side to keep the part straight. "Yes, it would be so much fun. I've always thought that I should try my hand at writing, but I've just never gotten around to it. Lloyd has encouraged me to do so, so maybe I will."

"Oh, that's exciting," I said. "I would love to read something you've written when you get a book finished."

She grinned. "Well, I'll tell you what, you can be my advance readers. I'd like to know if the story is any good before I try to publish it. Would you do that for me? Would you be my advance readers? Both of you?" She looked from me to Lucy and back.

"We would love to," Lucy said. "You just say the word, and we'll take a look at it."

She grinned. "Oh, you ladies are the best. Of course, I've got to write the book first." She laughed. "Look at me, talking about my book as if it already exists and I haven't even begun it yet. I have so many ideas, I'll have to figure out which one I want to begin with."

"I'm sure that's every writer's problem," I said. "Figuring out which story to work on. Well, Janet, we've got to get going, and we will see you tonight."

She nodded absently, still thinking about her book. "See you ladies later."

We headed back out to my car, and when we got inside, I turned to look at Lucy. "Sounds like there's a little drama going on at the book club."

She chuckled. "You can say that again. Oh well, we'll have to get the details tonight."

I started the car. I could do without the drama, but where there were two or more people, drama would follow.

CHAPTER 3

After we checked out the library book, we stopped by the grocery store to pick up a few things. I still wasn't completely certain about what I was going to make, so I grabbed a variety of ingredients and brought them home. It's not like I wasn't going to use them all eventually, anyway.

"What are you going to make?" Lucy asked as she dragged a chair from the table over to the kitchen island and made herself comfortable.

I shook my head as I put a pot of coffee on. "I'm thinking cream puffs. How does that sound?"

"Oh, that sounds delicious. I haven't had a good cream puff in ages. I predict they will be a hit."

I nodded as I opened my refrigerator and looked inside. "I'm thinking biscotti too."

"I love biscotti. Especially since there's going to be coffee there, it's a brilliant choice."

I closed the refrigerator and went to my cupboard. "I could also make some cupcakes. Everybody loves chocolate, don't they? Oh, except for those with allergies. Maybe I should skip the chocolate." I wanted to make a good impression at the book club. I don't know why, because there would be plenty of other treats. Even if I made something that wasn't so great, would anyone really notice? Oh, who was I kidding? I had a reputation in this town. If I made a flop of a dessert, people would talk.

Lucy opened the book and began turning the pages. "It's exciting that we're reading a book written by a resident of Sandy Harbor. I wish I could write. I would love to make up characters and events and put them together in a book."

I nodded absently as I looked through my cupboard. "Me too. It would be a lot of fun. You could write about people you know and thinly disguise them while laying out their misdeeds on the page." I chuckled. I didn't know if authors did that, but it was fun to think about.

Lucy chuckled. "Right? Oh."

When I turned to look at her, her eyes were wide. "What?"

"Do you suppose that's what Lloyd did? He wrote

about people in this town, but disguised their true identity? And it's all here in this book." She held up the book and gave it a little shake. "Maybe the town's secrets are about to be exposed."

I stared at her, and then I laughed. "Don't be so dramatic, Lucy. What kind of secrets do you think people have around here?" And then I thought about it. "I forgot, this is Sandy Harbor. You're right. Get reading. We've got to see if any secrets are exposed."

"I knew Lloyd years ago."

I turned back to her. "And?"

She shrugged. "He was a little strange. He was always asking questions about, well, everything. It was when Ed and I were newly married and we couldn't afford a washer and dryer, so we had to use the laundromat. It seemed like he was always there when we were, and he was always asking questions. Like, why were we there instead of buying our own washer and dryer? Where did we work? Did we have kids?" She shook her head. "It got on my nerves, and I told Ed he needed to say something to him about minding his own business, but he wouldn't do it. You know Ed. He doesn't like confrontation."

I nodded. "Maybe Lloyd was gathering information for his books."

"That's what I'm worried about."

I narrowed my eyes at her. "Why? What do you have to worry about? Do you have secrets?" I teased.

She shrugged. "Like I said, I got tired of his questions, and I may have gotten just a little snippy with him. What if he writes about a character who is gorgeous and young, but she's snippy with everyone? Then for sure, I would know that he based that character on me."

I laughed. "Lucy, you are something else."

"What? You don't think I'm gorgeous?"

I kept laughing and shook my head. "Of course, I think you're gorgeous, Lucy. You're my best friend. What else would I think about you?" Lucy and I had become fast friends when I moved to Maine with my first husband years ago. I couldn't imagine my life without her. "I think I'm going to make cream puffs and raisin and almond scones. Forget the biscotti. I don't want to mess with the double baking. How does that sound?"

"Sounds great. You get to baking, and I'll get to reading."

She opened the book to the first page and began. "In the waning light of an autumn day, the ancient oaks and elms of the Grantham estate cast elongated shadows over the rolling lawns, a spectral dance of dark against the lush green. The manor, an edifice of stone and history, stood as a silent sentinel over a pastoral scene, its windows reflecting the dying embers of the sun with a melancholy glow. Within its venerable walls, the air was thick with the scent of aged parchment and the faint, lingering aroma of sandalwood—a testament to the generations that had dwelled within, each leaving a layer of memory and dust.

"Amidst this setting, Ellen Grantham wandered through the corridors of her ancestral home, her steps soundless on the Persian rugs that adorned the floors. The portraits of her ancestors gazed down upon her, their eyes imbued with the weight of expectation and the somber knowledge of their own mortality. Ellen, however, bore their scrutiny with a grace that belied her inner tumult, her mind a tempest of thoughts that fluttered like the leaves outside, caught in the autumnal breeze.

"As she paused before the grand window of the drawing room, the landscape before her seemed a painting from another era, untouched by the passage of time or the influence of modernism. Yet, she knew the illusion was just that—an ephemeral moment soon to be swept away by the inexorable tide of change. It was here, in this moment of reflection, that Ellen's story began—a tale of legacy, of the delicate balance between honoring the past and forging a future, a narrative woven from the threads of history and the vibrant hues of the human condition."

She looked up at me. "Say, that's not bad. He uses lots of big fancy words, but it's not terrible."

I nodded absently as I gathered the ingredients for the scones and placed them on the kitchen island. The scones wouldn't take long, but the cream puffs would take time to put together. "Not bad." I went back to the cupboard, got out two mixing bowls, and set them on the island.

Continuing on, she said, "Ellen's contemplation was interrupted by the sound of the grandfather clock in the hall striking the hour, its chimes resonant within the stone walls, a reminder of time's unyielding march. She turned from the window, her silhouette a ghostly figure against the backdrop of twilight. The evening's task awaited her, a duty born from tradition yet imbued with a personal quest for understanding.

"Descending the staircase, her hand grazed the banister, polished to a sheen by generations of similar caresses. At the base, the entrance to the library beckoned, its door slightly ajar, the room beyond a sanctuary of wisdom and whispers of the past. Ellen entered, the soft light from the hearth casting shadows that danced with the flicker of the flames.

"Here, amidst the leather-bound volumes and

manuscripts, she sought the answers to questions unasked, a journey not of distance but of depth. The legacy of the Granthams was not just in the land and the bricks that built their home, but in the stories, decisions, and sacrifices entwined in the fabric of their history. Ellen, with a resolve steeled by the lineage she represented, was determined to add her chapter, to navigate the labyrinth of heritage with a torch of her own making," Lucy continued.

"Interesting." I could drizzle a thin, orange-flavored icing over the scones, and that would be the perfect accent to the raisins and almonds. I was getting excited about this baking. Why hadn't I thought to look around and see if there was a book club before now? I mean, we had a library; there had to be a book club, right? I shook my head as I brought the salt and baking powder to the kitchen island while trying to listen to Lucy as she read. "Lucy," I interrupted.

She looked up at me. "Yes?"

"Maybe I should make a third treat? Maybe I should make the biscotti?" My black cat, Dixie, sauntered into the room and rubbed against my legs.

She shook her head. "Laura said there would be plenty there to eat. You don't have to make enough of each item for everyone who will be there, just a half dozen or so."

I nodded, but I felt a little guilty. Shouldn't there be enough just in case everybody wanted a scone? And shouldn't there be a variety of food items? But I didn't want to look like I was showing off. "Okay then, I'll just make the scones and the cream puffs since there are two of us attending. We'll get the lay of the land, so I'll know better what to make next month."

She nodded and got back to reading.

I poured us a cup of coffee and brought it to her side of the island, along with some vanilla creamer.

"Thanks," she said as she turned a page. "Oh, will you look at that?"

"What?" I said as I went back to get my cup of coffee.

"Somebody wrote in the book. Can you believe that? This is a brand new book and somebody is writing notes in the margins. I hate when people do that to books."

I shook my head as I brought my cup of coffee back to the island and leaned over to glance at the book. "It's just rude. Nobody wants to pick up a library book with someone's notes in it." I poured some creamer into my cup and gave it a stir.

She squinted at the handwriting done in pencil. "Huh."

"What?" I asked, glancing at the book again.

"It says, *under the light of the full moon, the truth shall emerge from the shadows, revealing what hides in plain sight.*" She looked up at me. "What do you suppose that means?"

I shook my head. "I don't know. Maybe somebody from the book club checked it out, read it, made some notes, and then returned it already. They probably weren't even paying attention to where they made the notes."

She looked at the note doubtfully. "I suppose that could be it."

I went back to the other side of the island and measured flour into a bowl. "I can't wait for the book club meeting. It's going to be a lot of fun."

She nodded. "Me too. We'll get to visit with some folks and eat some treats and talk about books. I can't think of a more perfect evening."

I measured sugar into another bowl. She was right. This would be the perfect evening.

CHAPTER 4

When we got to the library, it was closed and most of the lights inside were turned off, just as Laura had said. County budget cutbacks had hit the library hard, and that meant fewer open hours. I tapped on the glass door with my key, and a few moments later, Janet Dixon rushed out of a back room. Her brow furrowed when she realized who was at the door, but she unlocked it for us anyway.

"So, you did come," she said looking us up and down.

"Good evening, Janet," I said, smiling. "We sure did."

"Wouldn't miss it for the world," Lucy said as we stepped inside. "Especially since we really crammed to read the book this afternoon."

Janet sniffed, making no move to allow us any further inside. "Most people say they'll join, but don't show up."

"We could hardly wait to come." I held up the box with the scones and cream puffs. "I brought treats."

"We worked hard all afternoon on treats for the meeting," Lucy said. "Well, Allie did the baking, while I read the book aloud. We didn't quite finish it, but we read most of it."

Janet's eyes went to the box, and then she looked at me, ignoring Lucy. "Oh. Okay, then. It's funny, but Laura didn't say anything to me about new members."

"Oh, I would have thought she would have mentioned us. You don't mind us joining you, do you?" I asked. Even though she hadn't seemed to mind when we talked this morning, she now seemed reluctant for us to join.

She shook her head, but she did seem a bit perturbed about us being here. "No, of course not. Come on in." She stepped back, allowing us to move away from the threshold.

"Oh, I love the smell of books," Lucy said as we allowed the door to close behind us.

Janet locked the door. "We're having book club in the meeting room back here."

We followed her into the back room where about

a dozen people stood around visiting. A nearby table was set up with treats and a large coffee pot. "I'll just put these treats over with the other food." I set the boxes down, opened the lid, and caught Laura's eye. She grinned and waved, hurrying over to us.

"I'm so glad the two of you could come. Look, you brought some treats. It would have been perfectly fine for you to come without them. Oh, look at those cream puffs. I've got to have one of those."

I smiled. "Nonsense. You know how much I love to bake. I made raisin almond scones with a lovely orange icing and the cream puffs."

She grinned. "Oh, I knew I could count on you to bring something absolutely delicious. But if you're ever not in the mood to bake, you can buy something from the grocery store. We won't complain." She laughed.

I liked Laura; she was always so bubbly and sweet. "And you know that is never going to happen."

Laura laughed again. "Of course not. What was I thinking? Why don't you ladies go ahead and have a seat, and we'll get started."

I nodded and we said hello to each of the other ladies as we took our seats. I knew everyone from around town, and there wasn't a stranger in the room.

"Why didn't we do this earlier?" Lucy leaned over and whispered.

I shook my head. "I don't know."

Laura stood at the front of the room. "I hope you ladies are doing well this evening. How about that book, huh? Did everybody get to finish it?"

There were nods around the room, and Laura sighed. "I tell you, I did finish it, but it was a chore. I hate to say anything negative about our book club pick, as you all know. But I found it difficult and hard going. Did anybody else feel the same?"

"Oh gosh," Janie Bridges said from the table next to ours. "I felt exactly the same way, Laura. The author just rambled on and on with descriptions of the trees and the bushes and the birds, and every little thing. And then in the next chapter, it would be more description about trees, and birds, and bushes." She rolled her eyes. "Oh well, what are you going to do? Not all books are created alike. This one was a real slog."

Laura laughed. "That's the perfect description of it. It was a slog of a book."

"I didn't like all the rough language," Adriana Bartle said from across the room. "Honestly, I've always felt that if you need to use foul language, then you have a very limited vocabulary. I don't know why authors have to do that."

She had a point. It did get old, especially since

Lucy was saying 'blank' each time she came to a naughty word.

"Well, I for one enjoyed the book," Patty spoke up. Patty Jackson was an older woman who was sitting at a table by herself in the back. "I thought his descriptions were enlivening. I could just picture the dogwoods and the blue jays. I can't imagine anybody not enjoying his descriptions. I happen to know Lloyd, and I know that he takes his writing very seriously. We are all very fortunate to have such a fine author living in our community." Her face lit up as she spoke about the book and author.

"I know him, too," Janet spoke up. "Lloyd Walker really has a way with words. This was one of my favorite books."

For a moment, Laura shuddered, but then she quickly smiled. "Oh, yes, we certainly are fortunate to have an author in our community. It's just that I could have done with a little less description of trees. I mean, I know that sort of description helps with the setting, but too much makes for difficult reading."

"You're wrong," Patty said. "I think it does the exact opposite. It gives you a feel for where the book is set, and makes you feel as if you are a part of it."

"That's exactly right, Patty," Janet said. "Lloyd did an excellent job placing his readers into the story. He has a real way with words."

Laura rolled her eyes. "Oh, please. The language was pretentious, as if he was searching for big words to impress someone. I have no idea who he thought he was impressing, but it wasn't me."

Adriana laughed. "Right? That's what I thought, too. So pretentious. I didn't know what half the words he used meant."

"Maybe you should invest in a dictionary," Patty suggested.

Adriana glared at Patty. "Maybe you should shut your mouth."

Lucy glanced at me, and I gave her a quick shrug of my shoulders. I mostly agreed with Laura, but the book did have its good points. There were several twists that I didn't see coming, and just when things seemed to be too long and drawn out, a twist would appear and renew my interest.

"Does anybody else have an opinion to share?" Laura quickly asked, looking around the room.

"I hated it," Susan Fisher said.

"I know Lloyd. He's as pretentious as his book," Pam Rollins said from the front. "Honestly, the book was a bore, and I knew it would be when Patty and Janet suggested it last month."

Patty gasped. "What? What are you talking about? It was a wonderfully engaging and enlightening book.

You don't know what you're talking about. None of you have any taste in literature."

Laura turned to Patty. "I think Pam has a point. I wasn't looking forward to this book, if you want to know the truth, and it was very difficult to get through. I don't understand why somebody needs to use the language that was used, and the book was just awful."

I was a little taken aback that Laura would say it like that when she knew that Patty and Janet obviously enjoyed the book as well as knew the author. I glanced back at Patty, and her cheeks had gone red as she folded her hands together on the table in front of her.

"Laura, that's not nice at all. If you knew Lloyd, you would understand how much hard work he puts into his books," she said, her voice sounding shaky now. "I've read everything he's written, and they are all excellent books. You don't have any right saying these things about him."

"I agree with Patty," Janet said through clenched teeth. "Lloyd Walker is a wonderful writer, and his book sure beats any of that romance trash we usually read."

Laura leaned on the podium. "You're right, Patty. I'm sure that Lloyd put a lot of work into his books. Now then, does anybody else have an opinion? And are there any specific examples that you can give of why you feel the way you do about it? Allie? Lucy? Did you ladies get a chance to read the book? I know it was such short notice, and I don't blame you if you couldn't make it through it."

"I thought it was a well-written book," Lucy said, glancing at me. "I would have liked to have had time to go through the book a little slower, but we didn't quite make it to the end."

I nodded. "Yes, I can see that Lloyd takes a lot of care in choosing the words that he uses." The truth was, I found my mind wandering while Lucy read. It was not a book that I would have chosen for my own personal reading.

We sat as everyone gave their opinion on the book, and I am afraid that no one really cared for it, except for Patty and Janet. As each negative review came in, they seemed to get more agitated. I felt sorry for them because they clearly enjoyed the book.

When the discussion ended, we got up and went to the dessert table, and I was delighted to see several homemade offerings as well as store-bought. "Adriana, did you make that cherry pie?" I asked.

She nodded. "I certainly did. I'm sure it can't compare to anything that you made, but I do enjoy a good cherry pie."

"Oh, now," I said. "I know it's going to be delicious, and I am going to have a slice of it."

"Laura, can I see you for a moment?" I overheard Patty saying.

Laura sighed. "Sure, what is it?"

The two of them moved over to a corner of the room, where a lively conversation ensued, although it was whispered. I glanced at Lucy, and she shrugged.

We helped ourselves to coffee and treats, and I cut myself a thin slice of the cherry pie and got a snickerdoodle cookie, and we went back and sat down at the table.

"The pie looks good. I should have gotten a slice," Lucy said, as she picked up a sugar cookie and dunked it into her coffee.

"It's delicious," I said, taking another bite. "The crust is light and flaky, and the filling is tasty with just a hint of cinnamon." It was nice letting somebody else do the baking now and then. Adriana did a great job with her pies.

"You've got some nerve," Patty said loudly. We all turned to look at her. Laura was grinning, shaking her head. "I'll have you know that Lloyd and I are friends, and he is a better writer than 99% of the writers out there."

Laura said something we couldn't hear, and then patted Patty's arm and turned back to the dessert table. "Oh wow, look at all of these goodies. We all outdid ourselves this month, didn't we?" She poured herself a cup of coffee while Patty stood there in the corner trying to gather herself. She looked as if she were on the verge of tears. I turned back to Lucy, and she looked at me, eyebrows raised.

"What do you suppose she said?" she whispered.

I shook my head. "I don't know." The atmosphere in the room had turned uncomfortable, and I felt sorry for Patty. It would have been nice if people could have given their opinions of the book a little more nicely than they had.

A moment later, Patty stormed out of the room.

CHAPTER 5

"So, what did you think of the book club?" Lucy asked, after we had run in silence for a while.

It was the following morning, and the air was colder than I had expected, even with the sun shining. "I think it was fun. I mean, other than the bickering, but even that wasn't terrible. I'd love to keep going. I'm going to be reading books anyway, and I'm going to be baking anyway, so why not? Why? Didn't you enjoy it?" I glanced at her as we ran down the running trail. She had been quiet this morning, and it made me wonder.

She gave a slight shrug of her shoulders. "I don't know. I was just wondering what you thought about it. It was fun, but to be honest, I really didn't care for the book much. They were right. It was long and drawn out, and all that description just got boring."

"Lloyd Walker has a way with describing scenery," I said. "But you're right, when there's too much, it's just boring."

"Pretentious."

I chuckled. "That's it. That's the word for it. Thad had Lloyd for ninth-grade English, and the two had butted heads. It seemed like Lloyd was always criticizing him. I felt like he was being too hard on him. I know, since I'm his mother, it made it hard for me to judge the situation, but I'm telling you, that Lloyd was something else." My son Thad was now a teacher at the high school, along with his wife, Sarah.

"Really?" Lucy said. "You didn't mention that Thad had him for an English teacher."

I nodded as we ran. "I forgot about it, to tell you the truth. Jennifer never had him as a teacher, and at the second semester, Thad changed classes."

"Well, I'm excited about our next book. And we'll have plenty of time to read it this time around."

"Me too. I love a good women's fiction book, and *All I Know* promises to be a good one." I read a variety of books, but some I enjoyed more than others. Women's fiction and mysteries were some of my favorites, and this next book was women's fiction with a touch of mystery. It looked to be a real winner.

She nodded. "I think it will be a lot of fun. Maybe we can give a few suggestions for books after we've settled in and become a part of the group."

"I bet they wouldn't mind." We ran on in silence again. It was early in the morning and with a little luck, we wouldn't see any more snow this year. I was more than ready to say goodbye to it, and it was quickly melting from the sides of the road. The thing about living where it snowed a lot was that late spring brought a lot of muddy, dirty snow as well as the growing flowers and budding trees.

"I did think Laura was being a bit harsh about Lloyd Walker and the book. It almost felt like she was trying to egg Patty and Janet on. Clearly, they enjoyed the book and since they know Lloyd, it seemed that they felt like they had to defend him." Lucy turned to look at me as we ran.

I hated to say it, but she was right. I liked Laura a lot, but it did seem like she was trying to be mean to Patty and Janet, and I couldn't understand why she would behave that way. "It did seem that way. I mean, just because she didn't like the book, she didn't have to say those things. What's wrong with saying that the book wasn't for you and maybe pointing out a few good things about the book? It's not like the book was absolutely horrible or anything. With the setting being in Maine, he did a good job describing it and making you feel like you were there. Or, rather, here."

"And he's a decent writer. The words really flowed, and it was good. I hope they can all get along because it felt rather awkward. Not to mention almost everybody sided with Laura, and I don't know if that was their true opinion of the book or if it was one of those things where they were ganging up on poor Patty and Janet."

I sighed. "I hope that's not the case. If it is, you would think Patty and Janet would have quit the book club long ago. I wouldn't stay someplace where I wasn't wanted." But some people didn't have sense enough to take the hint.

She nodded as we ran along. "I don't want to be a part of something where somebody is being picked on if that's the case. It's clear that Janet isn't happy with the book club since she thinks Laura got to be president because she got the others to vote for her. And I wonder what the conversation between Laura and Patty was about."

"We'll have to go to a few more meetings to try to get a sense of what's going on there. I'm with you; I don't want to be a part of something if someone is being picked on. There's no way I'm going to join in on something like that." I had had the unfortunate experience of being bullied in the third grade when new girl

Clarice Livingston decided that little redheaded me was going to be her target, and she did an amazing job of rounding up some of the meanest girls in the school and became the ringleader. I still can't understand how she managed to do it in such a short period of time, and I was glad when third grade was behind me and so was Clarisse. Her father got another job transfer and she was gone before the beginning of fourth grade.

We ran along for a bit, and the breeze picked up. It was suddenly chillier than it had been when we started our run, and I wished I had brought a heavier jacket.

I was just about to say something to Lucy about the cold when I glanced further down the trail and saw that there was something lying there. "What's that?"

Lucy looked in the direction I was pointing and squinted. "I don't know. It looks like… someone."

I nodded. "Maybe they're having a medical situation." We ran faster, and the closer we got, the more I could see that it indeed was a person lying there. I wondered if they had fallen and hurt themselves, or maybe they had had a heart attack of some sort, but I could see that they weren't moving.

We pushed ourselves to run faster. I didn't see anybody else out on the trail, but there were a lot of bushes and trees, so we might come upon somebody else that could help.

We were breathing hard and running full out by the time we got to the person lying on the ground. To my horror, I realized it was Laura Landers. "Laura!" I cried as we came to a stop in front of her. Laura didn't move, and even more horrifying was the fact that there was blood on her shirt.

"Oh, no!" Lucy breathed out in a gasp.

I kneeled beside her. "Laura! Laura!" But she still didn't move. I pulled my phone from my pocket and hit the dial on my husband Alec's number. I reached over and grabbed her wrist, but she was cold. "Oh no." After a moment, Alec answered the phone. He had chosen to sleep in late instead of getting up and going for a run this morning before going to work.

"Hello?" he said sleepily.

"Alec," I gasped. "Alec."

"Allie? What's going on? Why are you breathing so hard?"

"Alec, you need to come down to the running trail. Laura Landers has been shot." I glanced at the blood on her shirt. I had no idea if she was shot or not, but since I didn't see a knife protruding from her chest, I decided the blood had to have come from a bullet wound.

"Is she still alive?" he asked, sounding more alert now.

I shook my head even though he couldn't see it. "No, I don't think she is. She's cold, and I can't find a pulse."

"Is there anybody else around? Do you think the shooter is still there? You need to find someplace to take shelter."

"It's quiet out here, and I don't see anyone."

"I'm calling an ambulance, and I'll be right there. Find someplace to hide."

He hung up, and I looked up at Lucy. "He's afraid the shooter might still be around here, and he wants us to find someplace to hide." I glanced around as I spoke, but there was no one in sight.

"I think we're safe here," she said. "Oh, poor Laura. How awful." She shook her head and looked away.

I nodded. "The poor thing." Even though Alec wanted us to find someplace to hide, I didn't want to leave Laura. I felt her wrist again, searching for a pulse but still couldn't find one. If she was still alive, I wasn't going to leave her alone. I wanted her to know that we were here. "Laura? Laura, can you hear me?"

Laura didn't make a move, and my heart sank. Who would want to kill Laura? And then Patty and Janet came to mind.

CHAPTER 6

"I hate leaving her like that," Lucy said.

"Me too, but we can't move her. Alec will be here any minute, and he'll know what to do." Laura was lying near an entrance off of a street on the running trail, and she was out in the open. She lay sightless, looking up at the sky, and I had to look away. Here lay the bubbly and vivacious young woman that nearly everyone in town knew and loved. It would have been hard to find anyone who said anything negative about her. Well, other than Janet Dixon and Patty Jackson. I hated to leave her lying here out in the open, but there was no way I was going to touch her until Alec got here to look her and her surroundings over.

We were sitting on a bench on the side of the

running trail, hoping no one would come down the trail before Alec got here. "It seems like somebody would have heard her get shot," Lucy said after we had sat in silence for several minutes.

I glanced around. The houses in the neighborhood all sat back quite a way from the walking trail. But still, wouldn't somebody have heard something? "I can't imagine how no one heard the shot and yet nobody called it in. It's a nice neighborhood, so it's not like they're accustomed to hearing gunshots."

She nodded. "Exactly. If I heard gunshots in my neighborhood, I'd be on the phone so fast your head would spin."

"Me too."

I glanced up and saw Alec's car speeding down the street toward us. He parked at the entrance to the running trail and jogged the short distance to where Laura lay. We got up and walked over to him.

He knelt down, and checked for a pulse, then shook his head. "She's been gone for a little while."

I wrapped my arms around myself. I had suddenly grown cold. "The poor thing. I can't imagine who would do something like this to her. It's a gunshot wound, isn't it? It looks like one."

"There's no knife, so it's got to be a gunshot wound. Doesn't it, Alec?" Lucy asked.

Without glancing at us, he took a closer look at

Laura's eyes. "Probably, but we won't know for sure until the autopsy." He took his phone out of his pocket and began taking pictures. "I need you both to step back, please. There will be more officers on the scene in a few moments."

Lucy and I took several steps back, but we continued looking around the ground near Laura's body. There had to be something left behind.

"We haven't seen any shell casings," I told him. "Wouldn't you think there would be a shell casing? And how does somebody manage to hit her in the heart with one shot?" I may have been guessing at her being shot in the heart, but if it wasn't in the heart, it certainly was close.

He glanced at me and continued taking pictures. "Lots of people are good shots, Allie. It wouldn't be hard to do. And as for the shell casing, they may have collected it, so there would be one less piece of evidence for us to track them down."

I knew he was right about the killer probably being a good shot. I just couldn't come to terms with the fact that Laura Landers was dead. We had just spoken to her the night before, and for someone who was so full of life to suddenly have lost that life—it was a shock.

"What kind of a gun do you think it was, Alec?"

Lucy asked. "It couldn't be a shotgun, right? That would make a really big hole."

"Uh-huh," he said absently, without looking at us. "Won't know until the autopsy."

I heard sirens in the distance, and within a few moments, they arrived, parking behind Alec's car. With the sound of the sirens filling the neighborhood, people began to move the curtains in their windows and peek out, and an elderly woman stepped out onto her front steps. It wouldn't take long before there were going to be all sorts of looky-loos hanging around.

Yancy Tucker was the first officer out of his car, and he walked quickly over to Alec and squatted down beside him. Alec whispered something to him, and he looked up in our direction. I nodded and smiled at him. He nodded back, and they returned to talking. Two more police officers trotted down the short length of the trail to Alec's side.

"How long until we get asked to leave?" Lucy asked, leaning over.

I shrugged. "Shouldn't be long now."

I looked back in the direction we had come from, and I saw a lone runner headed toward us. I nudged Lucy, and she shook her head. "Whoever that is, is going to get the surprise of their life."

"Alec," I hissed. "Alec!"

Alec looked at me, and I nodded my head in the lone runner's direction. He frowned and said something to one of the officers, who stood up and turned toward the lone runner. It was a woman with dark brown hair. The officer walked down the trail toward her, and when she realized something was going on, she increased her pace until the officer said something to her.

"That's Adriana Bartle," Lucy said.

I nodded. "Poor thing. She and Laura were close friends. This is going to break her heart."

"Who is that?" Adriana asked the officer, nodding in Laura's direction.

He shook his head, but he had his back to us, so we couldn't hear what he said to her.

She looked past him, and that was when she recognized Laura. "Oh, no. No! No, don't tell me!" She sidestepped around the officer and started running toward Laura.

"Adriana, don't do it," I said, stepping into her path.

She stopped in front of me. "Allie, please tell me it isn't so. Please tell me that isn't Laura. What happened? What's going on? Is she okay?"

I shook my head, reluctant to say the words. "Adriana, it's better that you don't go down there." We were only a few yards from where Laura lay, but the two officers had stepped in between her and us.

Tears sprang to her eyes, and she shook her head slowly. "No. It can't be so. What happened to her? Were you here? Did you see?" She looked at Lucy and then back at me.

"We were just out for our morning run, and we happened upon her," Lucy explained gently. "I am so sorry." She reached out and gave her arm a squeeze.

Adriana dragged her fingers through her hair, brushing it out of her eyes. "Oh my gosh. I can't believe this. She's really gone? How could that have happened? Could you tell what happened to her?"

Lucy and I glanced at each other. I didn't want to give away more than I should. "The police are handling the investigation. My husband Alec is here, and he'll figure out what happened to her." There. I didn't have to lie.

Tears rolled down her cheeks as she shook her head, trying not to look at Laura's lifeless body. "This is horrible. I can hardly stand it. Her husband will be broken-hearted, and her son will be devastated. How could this have happened? Was there anybody else here in the area when you found her?"

I shook my head. "No, we didn't see anyone. I'm so sorry for your loss, Adriana. I know this is devastating. Alec will get a hold of her husband and talk to him though." I hoped that she wouldn't go and break the news to him. It was something that was best left to professionals.

"Can I have a word with you?" Alec said, coming up behind us. "I'm Detective Alec Blanchard."

She nodded. "I just can't believe this."

He pulled out a little notebook from his coat pocket. "Can I get your name?"

She nodded. "Adriana Bartle. She's really dead?"

He nodded. "I'm afraid so. What was your relationship to Laura?"

"We've been best friends since third grade. We did everything together."

Alec jotted down a note as the coroner's van pulled up.

"When was the last time that you saw her?"

"At the book club last night. Allie and Lucy were there. They saw her too. We were all having such a great time last night. I just can't get over this." A tear slipped down Adriana's cheek, and my heart went out to her. Losing someone she had been close to for so many years was tough.

Alec nodded and glanced at us. "I'll talk to the two of you later. You can go ahead and go."

We nodded. "Adriana, I'm so sorry," I repeated. "We'll get in touch with you in a few days and check up on you."

"I'm so sorry for your loss," Lucy said, and patted her shoulder.

Adriana sniffed. "That's sweet of you ladies. I'll talk to you later."

Lucy and I headed back up the trail, and I glanced over my shoulder at Alec. He gave me a nod, and we continued on back to my car.

"That's so sad," Lucy murmured.

"Isn't it though?" I didn't know who would kill someone as sweet as Laura, but we would figure it out.

CHAPTER 7

"Oh, somebody's going to be walking soon," Lucy said in a sing-song tone.

"She took three steps the other day and refuses to repeat it." I eyed my beautiful granddaughter, Lilly, as she maneuvered her way around the living room, holding onto the chairs and couches. Lilly had a mind of her own and at fourteen months had decided to keep us all in suspense. She wasn't going to walk just yet.

Lucy shook her head and took a sip of her coffee. "The girl is going to do things her way, and there's no use trying to get her to do it any other way." Lilly looked over her shoulder at Lucy and grinned, giving a little chuckle. "See what I mean?"

I nodded and took a sip of my coffee. "I know. And

I'm probably crazy for wanting her to get on with walking anyway. She's going to get into everything and I'm going to have to chase after her to make sure she doesn't hurt herself." A baby's first steps is a milestone in their lives, as well as the lives of their parents. I had been thrilled and excited when my own kids had gone from being crawlers to walkers. Sure enough, I soon regretted it as they ran through the house, laughing gleefully, grabbing things off shelves, and shoving things to the floor. But it had been an exciting and happy time in our lives. If Lilly wanted to take a little extra time to get on her feet, then I was going to be happy about it.

Lucy nodded. "She's going to be up to all kinds of shenanigans once she gets good at walking."

"Right? I can hardly wait though." I took another sip of my coffee and looked at her. "I still can't get over the fact that Laura was murdered."

She winced. "I still can't get over the fact that we're the ones who found her. The poor thing. Her family is going to be devastated, not to mention her friends. I really can't imagine who would have wanted to do something like that to her."

I sighed. "She's the last person I would have thought somebody would want to murder. She was one of those people who seemed to really have her life together. People really liked her. But somebody wanted her dead, and that makes me wonder about all kinds of things."

She looked at me with one eyebrow raised. "What do you mean?"

I shrugged. "I'm just saying that somebody wanted her dead, and they made sure it happened. There's a reason for it, and I want to know what it is." Lucy and I had unofficially helped investigate a murder case or two, and it had become sort of a hobby for us. Alec had come to expect it and didn't complain. Or at least he didn't complain much.

"You're right. Something must have been going on in her life that we are completely unaware of. Maybe that niceness she always displayed was an act." She narrowed her eyes in thought. "Maybe she was really mean to people she didn't consider important."

I hated to think that Laura had faked her kindness, but some people were good at pretending to be something they weren't.

The front door opened and closed, and a moment later Alec stood in the living room doorway. It was after eight o'clock in the evening, and Lucy had come over to sit with me as we commiserated over having found Laura Lander's body. My son Thad and his wife Sarah had stayed at the high school for a meeting and then were going out to dinner afterward. They would be by later to pick Lilly up.

"You look tired," Lucy said to Alec.

He nodded and scooped Lilly up into his arms. She laughed gleefully, and he planted a kiss on her forehead. "I am exhausted. But looking at this little lady, I might be able to muster a little extra energy to play with her."

"Thad and Sarah will be by shortly to pick her up," I said. "Have you eaten? I can whip something up for you."

He shook his head. "We ordered pizza at the station a couple of hours ago. I'm fine."

Lucy glanced at me. "Well, I had better get going. Ed is going to send out a search party if I don't show up pretty soon."

I chuckled. "You had better check in with him before he does that."

She got to her feet and picked up her purse. "I'll talk to you in the morning, Allie. Take care of yourself, Alec. And that baby."

"I sure will, Lucy. Have a good evening." He came over and sat next to me while Lucy showed herself out.

"Well? What's going on?" I asked.

He shrugged as Lilly took hold of his watch and tried to pull it off his wrist. "You know how it is. It's too early to know anything yet. Lilly, you can't have that."

Lilly pulled the watch to her and put her mouth on it.

"What about her husband? And her family? Doesn't she have kids?"

"She has one son who is away for his first year of college in Oregon. He's going to take the next plane home. Her husband is devastated, as you can imagine, and doesn't have any idea who would want to kill his wife." He gently extricated the watch from Lilly's mouth and took it off his wrist, placing it between the couch cushions where she couldn't get at it. She made a sound of protest, and he tapped her on the nose, distracting her.

"Where was he this morning? At work?"

"No, he was out fishing."

I narrowed my eyes at him. "What do you mean, fishing? It's the middle of the week. Was he by himself? Does he have an alibi?" I was ready to pounce on Derrick Landers being the killer. He seemed as nice as Laura had been, but the spouse was always the first suspect.

He chuckled. "He's on vacation this week, and he and a buddy are spending the majority of the week fishing. The ice has melted on the lakes, and you know how the fishermen around here are this time of year."

I sighed. "Watching the ice melt on the lakes is

practically an Olympic sport around here this time of year. I don't see the appeal of fishing. But his alibi holds up?"

He nodded. "He was with Dennis Crane, and he swears he was there with him the whole time."

"Wait, they were camped out at one of the lakes? It's freezing at night. RV or tent?"

He shook his head. "No, he said they drove out early in the morning. The ice officially broke last week, so they've been going fishing every morning and staying all day. I couldn't find him at home, so I talked to his boss. Had to go hunting for them at the lake to tell him what had happened."

"What awful news to receive."

He nodded. "It's awful to give that news too." Lilly pulled herself up by holding onto the front of his shirt and stood, one foot on each of his legs.

"Lilly, if you're going to stand up, then you may as well walk." I couldn't help myself. I wanted to be patient about her walking, but I also wanted to see her walk. I needn't have bothered saying anything, though, because she just ignored me and wrapped her chubby little arms around Alec's neck.

Alec grinned. "There's my big girl."

I tickled her ribs, but she ignored me. "Her husband has an alibi, so he can't be the killer, then.

Did he have any idea who might have wanted to do this?"

He shook his head. "No, he was devastated, and he had no idea who might have wanted to kill her. So unfortunately, I don't have any leads right now."

I put my feet up on the coffee table. "There were no shell casings, and nothing to lead to the killer. Now what?" Once I got thinking about a murder, I couldn't stop.

"We're hoping to get a report from the coroner within a couple of days to verify what kind of bullet, but so far I don't have anything to go on. I'll keep talking to people." Lilly squealed, then pinched his nose. They both laughed, and he turned to me. "We found a knit beanie beneath one of the benches. We're running analysis on it, but we don't know if it belongs to the killer."

"Interesting. Does it look like it belonged to a man or woman?"

He shrugged. "It's black. It could belong to either."

I sighed. I hated not knowing anything about who might have killed Laura Landers. A woman like that would have had far more friends than enemies, and for some reason, this fact made me even more intrigued about who might have killed her. We were going to get to the bottom of this, if it was the last thing we did.

CHAPTER 8

Finding out that someone you have known for years has been murdered is a shock. But actually finding the body of said person is horrifying. I couldn't imagine who would want to kill Laura Landers. The cute, perky blonde was sweet as honey and pretty as a picture. But there was one person who I was sure had to know something about the murder, and that was her best friend, Adriana Bartle.

"Poor Adriana. She was so upset yesterday," Lucy looked out the window as I drove over to the clothing shop on Main Street where Adriana worked. Main Street Duds sold mid-priced clothing for the whole family and Adriana had worked there for several years.

I nodded. "Those two were close, and I can just imagine how devastated she must be right now."

"I bet she's feeling the same way I would feel if you were murdered," she turned to look at me.

I glanced at her from the corner of my eye. "Well, I appreciate the sentiment, but I don't have any intentions of being murdered."

"Good. I'd hate to have to go through that. And poor Alec would be devastated."

I nodded as I pulled into a parking space in front of the clothing shop. When I turned my car off, I turned to her. "Just make sure you solve my murder. If I do get murdered, I mean. I don't want my murderer out running around and enjoying their lives, while I'm rotting in a grave somewhere."

She made a face. "Don't say that. I don't even want to think about it."

I nodded again, and we got out of the car. With a police detective for a husband, I felt reasonably sure no one would be dumb enough to come after me. I may have been making a big mistake thinking that, but Alec would hunt down my killer and wouldn't rest until they were behind bars. It would be a foolish mistake for someone to kill me.

We walked into the clothing store and inhaled the scent of new clothes. All the spring fashions were hanging from the racks, including bathing suits, both bikinis and maillots. It was far too chilly for bathing suit season, but the clothing stores didn't care. It was all about making a buck.

Adriana was hanging children's bathing suits on a rack near the center of the store. There were several other shoppers looking over the merchandise hanging from the racks, and another salesperson straightened a display of fall sweaters, now forty percent off.

We headed over to Adriana, and when she saw us, she smiled sadly. "Good morning, ladies. How are you doing?"

I nodded. "We're doing as well as we can be after what happened," I said. "Adriana, how are you holding up? I know this has got to be devastating for you."

"Allie and I were just talking about how devastated we would be if we lost one another," Lucy said. "We know Laura held a special place in your heart."

She sighed and dropped the bathing suit she was holding back into the box on the cart in front of her. "I just don't understand it. We talked the night before, and we planned to go running together. But then she texted me later saying she had some errands to run, so she was going to go earlier than we normally did. I would have expected her to have already finished her run by the time I got there."

"Oh?" I said. "The two of you went running together? Lucy and I do too."

She nodded, her arms resting on the box of bathing suits in front of her. "Yes, we tried to run together as much as possible, but sometimes we weren't able to do it. I just wish I had decided to get up earlier and go with her. Maybe she wouldn't be dead now."

"You can't blame yourself," Lucy said. "You don't know what happened, and if you had been with her, the killer may have killed you, too."

"Yes, we might have been grieving two people today instead of just one." It was a normal response to blame oneself in a situation like this, but it would only make her feel worse to do it.

She sighed. "You're probably right. But I just can't let it go. Does Alec have any idea who might have killed her yet?"

I shook my head. "These things take time. But believe me, he is focusing on this case, and he will do his best to solve it as quickly as possible."

She nodded, looking away. "Of course. I know he's an excellent detective and he will find her killer. Has he talked to her husband?"

I knew that Alec had already talked to her husband, but I wasn't going to give out any information. Keeping my mouth shut was something I had learned to do since meeting Alec. "Yes, I know that he's talked to him, and as you can imagine, he's grieving terribly."

She gazed into my eyes and then nodded. "Yes, of course. I'm sure he's grieving." But she said it as if she wasn't so sure.

"Is there something you wanted to say?" I asked after a moment. If she knew something about Laura and her husband, I wanted to know what it was.

She shrugged and glanced away. When she looked at me again, there were tears in her eyes. "Laura was my best friend. We met in the third grade, and we were best friends ever since. I just don't know what I'm going to do without her. She started dating Derrick when we were seniors in high school. He was one of those boys who liked to show off. Always bragging about the new things his parents had bought for him. For his sixteenth birthday he got a brand-new car. I don't know what that thing cost, but I'm sure it was a pretty penny. He's never changed. Everything is always about him. I don't know how Laura put up with him for as long as she did."

"He came from money then?" I asked.

She nodded. "He was one of the most popular boys in school, and any girl who landed him was going to be envied. Well, Laura landed him, but I'm not sure there was much to envy."

A chill rushed down my spine. "What do you mean by that?"

She shook her head. "He was kind of a jerk. Always has been. He pushed her around, not that I mean he ever physically hurt her, but verbally. He always got his way when we were younger. But as we grew older, Laura learned how to handle him, and I'm afraid in her efforts to stand up for herself she kind of became this overbearing, pushy woman. She wasn't like that when we were in school, but he made her become that way."

I was surprised to hear this about Laura. She was always so bubbly and vivacious. It never would have occurred to me that she might be overbearing or pushy. "You're sure things never got physical between the two of them?"

She nodded. "I'm sure she would have told me if it had. We told each other everything, and I would have made sure she left him if he ever laid a hand on her. But she would yell at him, call him names, and threaten to leave him if she didn't get her way, and he always gave in. It was kind of strange to watch them swap roles. He had been that way in the beginning, but he sort of caved when she stood up for herself."

I wasn't sure what to make of all this. Alec had said her husband had an alibi, but I wasn't going to tell Adriana this in case the alibi fell through. "Do you think that he would have hurt her eventually? If it never came to blows before, do you think he would suddenly kill her?"

She hesitated, her cheeks flushing pink. "I've been thinking about it all day yesterday and all last night. I didn't sleep a wink. I probably should have called in because I'm just exhausted, but all I could think about was Laura. Being here at work takes my mind off things, though. Yes, if they were arguing, I do think he could have lost control and killed her."

"But she was found out on the running trail," Lucy pointed out. "He would have had time to cool off if he went there and killed her."

She nodded. "Yes, you would think so, wouldn't you? But she said that he was going to go running with her. That was part of the reason I didn't want to get up early and go for a run with her. She told me she was going to be with him, and I would rather just skip all that drama, so that's why I went later."

I was surprised to hear this. If Derrick was there at the running trail with his wife, where had he been when his wife was killed? "Have you talked to him?"

She shook her head. "No, I haven't. I suppose I need to go over there and tell him how sorry I am for his loss, but I'm putting it off. I don't care about him and his loss. I only care about mine." She softened. "And her son's. I'm sorry for Jacob's loss."

I nodded. "Her son losing his mother at a young age is heartbreaking."

She sniffed and picked up a bathing suit out of the box again. "It really is. I'm just sorry Laura ever went out with Derrick, and even more sorry that she married him."

It was clear that Adriana didn't feel anything for Derrick, and I wondered how difficult that had made her relationship with Laura. I doubted she could have hidden her disdain for Laura's husband. What would something like that do to their relationship?

CHAPTER 9

*A*fter we had talked to Adriana at the clothing store, we headed over to the Cup and Bean coffee shop. I needed a strong shot of caffeine, and there was no better place in town to get it.

Our old friend Mr. Winters sat at a corner table, reading his newspaper with his little gray poodle, Sadie, sitting under the table with her pup cup. The dog was his dearest friend and cute to boot.

We hurried and got in the short line, and I gazed at the back of the man in front of us, thinking something about him looked familiar. Lucy elbowed me and nodded at the man, and I gave her a questioning look.

She mouthed something to me, but I didn't understand what she was trying to get across to me, so I shrugged. She put her thumb against her first and second fingers and wrote something in the air, but I shrugged my confusion again. Rolling her eyes, she placed her lips almost against my ear and whispered, "Lloyd Walker." Of course. How could I not have recognized the bald circle at the back of his head?

"Lloyd?" I asked. "Lloyd Walker?"

The man turned and looked at me and smiled. "Yes?" he said, trying to place us.

I smiled. "My goodness, to think we just ran into Lloyd Walker right here at the Cup and Bean Coffee Shop." I turned to Lucy. "Can you believe it?"

She shook her head. "No, I am so amazed. Mr. Walker, we just finished reading your book, *'The Sun Grieves'*, and it was wonderful. I can't get over the eloquence of your writing. It was fantastic. I just loved it," Lucy said.

Lloyd beamed. "Why thank you, ladies. That's very kind of you to say so. I, uh, didn't get your names."

We each introduced ourselves to him and shook his hand. "You probably don't remember me, but I remember when you were a teacher at the high school. You sure have come a long way." Flattery was my secret weapon. Rare was the person who didn't want to hear how wonderful someone believed they were.

He chuckled and nodded. "Yes, I certainly have.

I knew that my big break was coming any day now when I worked there, and it came." He thought for a moment. "Well, actually, I still work there. But it won't be long before I'm able to quit and write full time." We stepped up closer to the front counter.

"Oh, how I envy you," Lucy said. "You're living out your dreams."

"Oh gosh," I said. "A full time author? It's like I know a celebrity."

Lloyd laughed. "Oh, now you're going too far. I'm not a celebrity. Not yet. But maybe someday."

I shook my head. "I disagree. It's not many who have a real gift for writing like you do." Maybe we were laying it on thick, but I didn't know anyone else who had published a book before.

"Nonsense," he said. "I've just written a couple of books, and I got lucky with finding the publisher I did. They did all the hard work for me, putting the book together and the marketing."

"Well, I'm impressed," Lucy said. "We love to read, and it's fun getting to meet you."

He stepped up to the counter, placed his order, and then turned back to us. "Well, it was a lot of fun for me to get to meet the two of you."

"Can you sign my book?" Lucy said, whipping out the library copy of the book she had read while I baked scones. I gave her a wide-eyed look. That wasn't our book.

"Sure, I don't mind at all," he said, borrowing a pen from me. He opened the book and then looked at both of us. "This is a library book."

Lucy nodded. "Yes, we read it for our book club."

He frowned. "Book club? You mean that book club that meets at the library?"

I nodded. "Yes, that's the one. Say, we should have you come to our book club and do a reading for us. Would you do that? I know everybody would be thrilled to have you."

"What?" he said incredulously. "That's not what I heard. I heard you all hated my book."

I did my best to steady the look on my face and not give anything away. "What? Who told you that?"

His face went red. "What difference does it make who told me? I heard Laura Landers said my book was trash, and that everybody agreed with her. I have never been so insulted in all my life."

I shook my head. "No, we would never say that about one of your books."

He shoved the book back at Lucy. "You two are ridiculous. Sign your book, indeed. Don't waste my time."

"Oh, no, Lloyd, we really enjoyed your book," Lucy said. "Honestly. We were excited to get to read it."

"Oh yeah? That's why you're trying to get me to sign a library book? What good does that do you? You've got to turn it back in. I've never been so insulted in all my life. And I heard about that Laura Landers. Somebody killed her. Well, it serves her right. She's been running her mouth all over town about me and my book, telling everybody how awful it is. That's going to hurt my sales, you know. I've got bills to pay. How could she do something like that to me?"

I was taken aback by him saying Laura deserved to be murdered. "I'm sorry, I didn't realize she was talking to people around town about your book. You're right, she wasn't very nice about the book at the book club. But that's just one person's opinion, so what does it matter?" I asked, trying to smooth things over.

"I heard everybody was in agreement," he said, his bottom lip jutting out. "I heard everybody was mean and hateful about it. You would think people would be nice because I'm from Sandy Harbor and we should all support one another. But I guess those old hens down at the book club haven't got any decency about them."

"That's not true," Lucy said. "Janet Dixon and Patty Jackson were very supportive of your work. And so were we. You shouldn't take to heart what other people say about your work."

He shook his head. "What? Are you kidding me? Of course, I'm going to take to heart what people say about my work. Do you know how much work goes into writing a book? I pour my heart and soul into it, and then people just trash it like it's nothing? Of course I'm going to be angry about it. But the thing that makes me the angriest is that she went around town giving people her opinion, as if that was all that mattered." He turned his back on us just as the barista finished up with his coffee, and he picked it up and left, storming out of the coffee shop without another word.

Lucy and I stared at each other while the barista waited on us to take our orders. When I composed myself, we gave her our orders. I glanced at Lucy, and she was just as surprised by our encounter with Lloyd Walker as I was. When our coffee was done, we went over to sit with Mr. Winters.

"What's the matter with you two? You look like you've lost your best friend. But I'm still here." He laughed.

I shook my head. "We were talking to Lloyd Walker, the author, while we stood there in line, and he told us we insulted him, and then he stormed out of the coffee shop."

"He did? What did you do to him?" he asked.

I shook my head. "We didn't do anything. We told him we loved his book."

"Yeah, I even asked for an autograph," Lucy said.

"Well, you did ask for an autograph on a library book, and it's not like we were going to keep that library book," I pointed out.

Mr. Winters chuckled. "Maybe he thought you were making fun of him. I know Lloyd. He's a sensitive sort. But those writers always are."

I shook my head. "Did you hear about Laura Landers?"

He nodded. "Yeah, I heard she was shot at the running trail. Who would do something like that?"

I shook my head. "That is the question of the day. But apparently, she was spreading it around town that she couldn't stand Lloyd's new book."

"We went to our first meeting of the book club that meets at the library, and she did say that she didn't like it," Lucy told him. "And I mean, she *really* didn't like it. Lloyd said she was spreading it around town that she hated the book."

He took a sip of his black coffee and set his cup down. "Well, that wasn't very nice, especially if she was spreading it around town. But I don't care much for Lloyd Walker's books either. He's too long-winded, and he never gets to the point."

I sighed and took a sip of my coffee. We really hadn't meant to insult him, and I was still unsure how we managed to do it. But one thing was for sure, and that was that he was fully aware of Laura's dislike of his book. Why had she spread it around town that the book was awful? I glanced at the closed coffee shop door. Lloyd was awfully angry about it, and it made me wonder if he was angry enough to kill her over it.

CHAPTER 10

"The nerve of that Lloyd Walker, thinking we were spreading lies about him around town," Lucy said as she drove. "Just because Laura did it doesn't mean we would."

I shook my head. "You really can't blame him. I wish Laura hadn't spoken negatively about his book like she did. It's one thing to keep it in the book club, but to spread it around town was just uncalled for. Of course he's going to think that we were also speaking negatively about his book."

"I guess you're right," she sighed. "It just hurt my feelings to know that he thought we would run down his book like that. I mean, it wasn't the best book I've ever read, but it wasn't the worst either. There would be no reason for me to discuss the book around town with people if I didn't like it. I usually just move on from books I don't like and get the next one."

I nodded. "Yes, but would you have finished the book if it hadn't been for the book club?" Not that we had finished it, but we tried. But I knew how I would answer that question, and the answer would be no. It just wasn't interesting enough. But like Lucy said, it wasn't the worst book I had ever read, either.

She pondered the question for a moment, then shook her head reluctantly. "No, I guess I wouldn't have finished it. But I would have felt out of place if we hadn't tried to read as much as we could with that being all everybody was talking about. But as it was, we didn't discuss the book all that much. It was a little disappointing."

"I feel the same way. Are we going to go back?"

"Are you kidding me? Of course, we're going to go back. Everybody's going to be talking about Laura's death. Maybe somebody will have some information that will help Alec solve the case."

I nodded. "That's what I thought."

We pulled up to the county library, parked the car, and got out. There was no use hanging onto the book any longer, and I was hoping we could get some information from Janet Dixon.

"Wait," Lucy said, stopping.

"What?"

"Lloyd said someone told him everyone was saying awful things about his book at the book club. That means there's a spy among us."

I looked at the library door. "I think Janet or Patty would be a good guess."

She nodded. "There could be no other."

We continued across the parking lot, and I pushed open the door, and Lucy followed behind me. Three other library patrons were looking for books among the racks, and Janet was sitting at the desk behind the counter. She looked up when we walked in, and I smiled at her; she grimaced, whether because she was in pain, or whether she thought we were the pain, I didn't know. She got up and came to the front counter.

"Good morning, ladies. How are you two doing? What did you think about the book club? It was your first time, wasn't it? Oh yes, I think you told me that when you were here that night."

I nodded, resting my hands on the counter. "Yes, it was our first time, and we really enjoyed it." That was a lie. We didn't enjoy it that much because of the bickering, but that didn't mean that we weren't willing to give it another shot. "We thought we had better return the book before it slips our minds, and we don't get it back until it's overdue. I would hate to have a library fine."

Lucy handed her the book, and she opened it. "Yes, we don't want you to have a fine. I'll just check it right in, and everything will be fine." She chuckled. "Get it? Everything will be fine, and you won't get a fine."

Lucy and I chuckled. "That's funny," Lucy said.

It wasn't, but we didn't want to put her off. "Janet, did you hear about what happened to Laura?"

Her eyes met mine, as she scanned the book with the scan gun. "Yes. I'm still in shock about it. Is your husband on the case? I know he's a detective at the police station and that he's the best around. I certainly hope that he's on the case."

I nodded. "Yes, Alec is working the case. Lucy and I came across Laura's body that morning while on a run. It was awful."

Her eyes widened. "What? You found her? Was she... Was she already gone?"

I nodded. "I'm afraid so. I can't even tell you just how shocked and horrified we were to find her."

"We're still shocked and horrified," Lucy said, glancing around to make sure that nobody was close enough to overhear our conversation. "I'm sure you can imagine just how awful it was, finding her that way."

Janet nodded slowly. "Oh goodness. I certainly can't imagine how awful that must have been. Oh, it's just too terrible for words. Are the two of you all right? Do you feel all right? Or have you been scarred for life? I know I would be."

I inhaled before answering. "We'll be all right. I'm sure it will take us a little time to get over it, but we'll be fine."

"Yes, it will take a little bit of time," Lucy agreed. "It's so sad."

"Janet, do you have any idea who might have wanted to harm Laura?" I asked.

She shook her head slowly. "No. Like I said, I just can't imagine it. I mean, we're talking about murder here. Who would want to do something like that to her? As you could probably guess, I was not a fan of hers, but I never tried to hide that either. But murder? No one deserves that. Gosh, it's just too terrible for words."

I nodded seriously. "Yes, it really is too terrible. But it seems like if she was having trouble with someone, maybe she would have mentioned it. At the book club... I know we all had plenty of time to sit around and chat about things that were going on in our lives, and I just wondered if maybe she let something slip?"

She sighed and leaned on the counter. "Oh, that Laura. She loved to talk about herself. Believe me, *she* was her favorite subject, but she would never confide in me. As I said, I wasn't a fan of hers, and she wasn't a fan of mine. But now that you bring it up, there is one person who had a problem with her. And that was her so-called best friend, Adriana."

I was surprised to hear her say this. Adriana had been broken up when she had been out for her run and stumbled upon us and her best friend lying dead on the running trail. She seemed genuine in her grief when we talked to her at the clothing store, too. "What do you mean?"

She glanced around the library, but the other three patrons were busy looking for books. Turning back to me, she said, "They may have said they were friends, but I think it's closer to something like frenemies. That's the term for it when two people who purport to be friends really can't stand one another."

I nodded. "Yes, I'm familiar with the term. I didn't realize they didn't like each other." This information was surprising, too. I had always seen the two as inseparable.

She sighed. "Well, Laura was just using Adriana. Adriana's family has a lot of money, and Laura always flattered Adriana and tried to make her believe she was more important to her than she really was. She used her."

Lucy gasped. "Really? I never would have guessed."

Janet nodded. "Oh, yes. Laura only thought about herself. She always made us read books she wanted to read. She didn't care about anybody else's opinion on books, certainly not mine or Patty's. The only reason we got to read Lloyd's book was because I insisted, and because the book that she wanted to pick was all checked out."

This wasn't the information that I wanted. I didn't care about who decided on which book for the book club. "I see. You're saying that Laura used Adriana. In what way? Did she ask for money from her? Or?" I asked, hoping she would fill in the blank.

She nodded. "I don't think that she came right out and asked for money, but she made her needs and wants known, and Adriana always felt like she had to oblige her. And that's what she did. She bought her clothes and purses, and other things. One time, Adriana bought her a diamond tennis bracelet for her birthday after Laura pestered her about it for weeks. If you ask me, I think Adriana just tired of it all and killed Laura."

"But do you think that's a strong enough reason for her to kill her?" Lucy asked.

Janet hesitated. "Well, she would have to have a really good reason to commit murder, wouldn't she? And that reason would be that Laura bullied her. She had since they were kids. Always trying to control everything about the relationship and making Adriana look bad if she didn't cooperate with her." She shook her head. "She spread lies about her."

I wasn't sure if I believed this. I didn't think that Janet was lying; however, I wasn't sure if this was just her opinion of things, since she had already admitted that she didn't particularly care for Laura. And if it was true, would it be enough for Adriana to feel like she had to kill her over it? Unless there was something that set her off.

"Do you think that something happened between the two of them? Something recently?" I asked.

She gazed at me for a moment. "It seems like Adriana has poor self-esteem. She worries about what people say about her and Laura knew this. I overheard Laura tell Adriana that she would hate for it to get out that Adriana's husband was a drunk. By the look on her face, I would say that she would have been mortified if that information got out."

Lucy and I looked at each other, then I turned back to Janet. "It sounds like a volatile relationship."

She nodded. "Yes, that's exactly the way it seems to me, too."

This was interesting information, and while I couldn't swear that it was something that would blow the case wide open, it was worth keeping in my back pocket until I could find out more.

We left the library and I turned to Lucy. "Is it my

imagination or did Janet's attitude about the murder change?"

"I don't think it's your imagination. She seemed upset about Laura's murder in the beginning of the conversation, but she almost seems glad she's dead now."

Interesting. Interesting indeed.

CHAPTER 11

I would like to have said that we were closer to finding Laura's killer, but the truth was that we weren't, and it frustrated me. These were the thoughts that ran through my mind as I measured flour into a mixing bowl and then reached for the canister of sugar. Dixie was asleep on the kitchen rug as I worked in the early morning hour.

"Hey, what are you doing?" Alec asked, coming up behind me and wrapping his arms around me. He kissed the back of my neck.

"Baking cupcakes to take to Laura's husband and son." I knew both Derrick and his son Jacob well enough to drop by and tell them how sorry I was for their loss, and I hoped at least one of them would be in the mood to talk.

Alec released me and went to the coffee pot. "I told you that Derrick has an alibi, and his son was out of state."

I nodded as I grabbed a set of measuring spoons. "I know. But Derrick has to know something, doesn't he? Somebody who was harassing Laura or something she might have said that will lead us to the killer?"

He took a travel mug from the cupboard and removed the lid. "That's what I keep hoping, but so far, he hasn't come up with anything helpful. Honestly, I am surprised. Usually, the spouse knows something that's going on, even if they don't want to admit it. But Derrick seems to be telling me the truth."

I nodded and measured the baking powder into the bowl. "Exactly. I'm sure he knows more than he's letting on, and I intend to get to the bottom of it." It was how you approached the loved ones of a murder victim that made the difference. Cupcakes would help grease the wheels.

He poured coffee into the mug and then went to the refrigerator for the creamer. "Just be careful how you question him. He was pretty broken up about his wife being murdered."

I nodded. "Of course. I don't intend to grill anyone. At least not unless I feel like they're the actual killers." I gave him a wink. "I mean, if her husband is the actual killer since her son was out of town. Do you know anything new about the case?" I didn't know if Laura's husband had anything to do with her death, but I was going to find out.

Alec turned to look at me. "Did I tell you we got the results back from the coroner? The bullet was a 9mm and we're going with it most likely being shot from a handgun, since that would have been easier to hide from Laura, and also if someone was driving by."

I looked up at him. "Unless someone is going to pretend that they were trying to shoot a deer and they hit her instead. Not that they should be shooting deer this time of year, and certainly not in town."

"No, it wasn't a hunting accident." He put the lid back on his travel mug and came back over to me and kissed me. "I've got to get going. I'll see you tonight."

* * *

I BAKED THE CUPCAKES, and while they were cooling, Lucy and I went on a run. It only took me a few moments to frost a dozen cupcakes and pack them up in a box when we got back to the house, and then we headed over to Derrick Lander's house.

Derrick looked surprised to see us when he opened the door. "Good morning, Allie, Lucy."

I smiled sympathetically. "Good morning, Derrick. We just wanted to stop by and tell you how sorry we were about Laura. I was baking cupcakes, so I brought you some. I hope you like coconut."

He smiled. "I love coconut. That was kind of you to think of us. Would you like to come in?"

"We would love to," I said, and we followed him into the house. He offered us a seat on the couch, and he sat across from us.

Derrick was tall and thin, with dark brown hair. "I'm afraid Jacob isn't up to company this morning."

"I don't blame him," Lucy said. "I'm sorry for your loss, Derrick."

He shook his head. "I still can't get over it. Who would want to kill my wife? Laura was loved by everyone who knew her. I don't suppose Alec has any ideas yet?" He turned to me.

"I know he's working hard to find Laura's killer, and he isn't going to stop until he does. But if he has anyone in mind yet, he hasn't mentioned it." Derrick may have thought that everyone who knew Laura loved her, but I could think of at least two or three people who didn't. Patty, Janet, and Lloyd Walker.

He nodded. "Yeah, I figured as much. Whoever it is has to be lying low. I only wish I hadn't gone fishing that morning. Maybe I could have done something to prevent this." He looked away, clasping his hands together in his lap.

Although Derrick appeared to be sorry about his wife's death, I didn't see any signs of tears. I would have thought his eyes would have at least been red, but they weren't. "You can't blame yourself," I said. "Whoever did this was probably planning it for a while."

"And they planned how to get away with it too," Lucy added. "I'm sure that's why Alec and his team haven't found the killer yet. But don't you worry, they will."

He looked back at us and smiled sadly. "I appreciate that. I know the police will do everything possible to find her killer."

"Laura was out running early that morning," I said. "Did she usually go that early?"

He shook his head. "No, she usually went running with Adriana a little later in the morning. The two are best friends, and they did nearly everything together. Like the two of you." He smiled. "It's great to have good friends, isn't it?"

I nodded. "It certainly is. Lucy and I go running most mornings. Sometimes earlier than others, so our schedule isn't always set in stone. Do you know why Laura went running so early that morning?"

He shook his head. "No, she didn't say. Other than

she had some errands to run, I mean. She was always on the go, so there's no telling what she thought she had to take care of that morning."

I nodded, remembering that Adriana said Derrick and Laura didn't have the best relationship, and she hadn't wanted to go running with Laura because he was supposed to go with her. "You must have gone fishing early."

He stared at me for a moment. A look crossed his face, and then he smiled. "Oh yeah, my friend Dennis and I were up early and getting in our fishing time. We've been waiting all winter for the lakes to thaw, and we weren't going to miss a minute of it."

"Were you on vacation?" Lucy asked. "Or were you going to work afterward?"

He chuckled. "Yeah, I was on vacation. I know other people go to exotic places on their vacations, but I went to the lake to fish. Laura said I was crazy, and maybe I am. But I really enjoy my fishing, and it was fun just to get away with a good buddy and do some fishing."

"That sounds like fun. I mean, if I enjoyed fishing, which I don't," I said, with a chuckle. "But it's fun just to get away and spend time with your friends. Lucy and I try to do fun things now and then, just the two of us. We leave our husbands at home and enjoy ourselves."

"I don't know what I'd do if I didn't get some time away with Allie now and then," Lucy said. "Ed would drive me crazy."

He nodded. "Nothing made me happier than spending time with my wife, but like you said, we all need to get away once in a while."

"I don't like going running by myself, though," Lucy said. "I haven't been running as long as Allie has, and I don't feel like I would be safe running by myself."

His forehead furrowed. "Yeah, I told her I wasn't sure she should go running alone, but she insisted. She said if somebody came after her, she could outrun them. Well, she could have outrun them if they were just running, but unfortunately, they had a gun, and there was no way for her to outrun a bullet. But yeah, I know what you're saying, Lucy. I probably should have insisted that she go later when she could run with Adriana, but I wasn't thinking. And besides, Laura was a force to be reckoned with. When she wanted to do something, she was going to do it, regardless of whether I wanted her to."

I smiled. "Laura was one of the happiest, most vivacious women I have known."

This made him smile, and he nodded. "I know what you mean. When I met her in high school, I knew I had to make her mine. There was just something about her."

We sat and talked for a few more minutes, and then we excused ourselves. When we got back into the car, I turned to Lucy. "It sounds like he had no intention of going running with Laura that morning. I wonder why Adriana said that he was?"

She nodded. "She said that was the reason she didn't go running earlier with Laura. She didn't want to be around Derrick."

"And did you notice that when I asked about him going fishing, he looked a bit confused?" I started my car. "Like he momentarily forgot that was where he had gone that morning?"

She nodded. "I sure did. What was there to be confused about? Supposedly, he took off a week from work so that he could go fishing every morning. He's suspicious, if you ask me."

"I'm with you on that," I said as I started the car and pulled away from the curb. "There's something up with him, and we need to keep an eye on him."

I hated to think that Derrick had killed his wife, but something was going on with him, and I was going to get to the bottom of it.

CHAPTER 12

When investigating a murder case, you've got to make sure that you've looked at every angle. And we were just getting started. There was another person I wanted to talk to, and that was Patty Jackson. She and Laura had exchanged words the night of the book club, and I wondered if Patty would tell us what that was about. I packed up half a dozen coconut cupcakes, and we stopped by her house.

Patty lived in a cute yellow house with white trim. It was a modest house with brick planters out front. I could see something was planted there, but it was still a bit too cold for anything to bloom just yet. Whatever she had in there would liven up the place and make it even more adorable than it already was come warmer weather.

I knocked on her front door, and in a moment the door opened, and she peeked out. She looked a bit confused, and said, "Yes?"

"Patty, it's Allie and Lucy. We wanted to stop by and see how you were doing, and I brought you some coconut cupcakes. I hope you like coconut." I held up the box.

She looked at the small box in my hands and blinked. Opening the door wider, she nodded. "Yes, I do like coconut. That's kind of you to think about me. Would you like to come in?"

I nodded. "We'd love to."

Patty was still wearing her bathrobe, even though it was nearly noon by this time. We followed her into the living room and sat down on the loveseat while she sat across from us on the couch. "That was nice of you to come by. I don't get many visitors."

I placed the box of cupcakes on the coffee table between us. "Well, with what happened to Laura Landers, we thought it would be good to check in on you and see how you were doing. Since she was president of the book club and all."

"The murder has everyone on edge," Lucy said. "It seems people aren't safe just going about their business anymore."

A PINCH OF HOMICIDE

Patty frowned. "I certainly hope the police are working to find her killer. We can't have killers just running around town murdering whoever they want."

I nodded. "My husband is on the case, and he's going to find the killer and put them away for good. Sandy Harbor has always been a nice little town, and there's no way that he would allow a killer to wander around scot-free."

She nodded, satisfied with my answer. "Good. The Sandy Harbor I grew up in was never a violent place, and I expect we will get back to that again."

"I agree," Lucy said. "We need this town to get back to what it was when I was a kid, too. It wasn't violent then either."

She sniffed. "It seems the older you get, things change, and you long for what you once had. But I don't like change, and I refuse to accept it."

I smiled. "I don't blame you. Change is hard. How have you been, Patty?" I didn't know how she expected to keep change from happening.

She nodded, pulling her robe tightly around herself. "I'm doing fine. I got up late this morning though, and haven't gotten much done yet. That's what happens when you stay up late watching a murder mystery marathon on TV." She laughed. "I told myself I wasn't going to stay up past 11:00, but it was nearly 3:00 AM by the time I got to bed. I guess that will teach me to stay up so late."

I smiled. "I know what you mean. I get caught up in marathons on TV too, and it's hard to shut it off and go to bed."

Lucy nodded. "Oh, I love a good mystery marathon. My husband Ed doesn't like them, but I sure do."

Patty crossed her arms in front of herself. "What does your husband say about the murder? Does he know who did it? I already know why she was killed, but I want to know who did it."

I shook my head. "No, he doesn't know who did it yet. What do you mean, you know why she was killed?" If we knew the why, it might lead us to the who.

She snorted. "Because Laura Landers was an awful person. She was hateful and thought she was better than everyone else. That's what happens when you grow up with money and you're pretty. It turned her into a hateful, awful person."

I did my best to hide my surprise at this statement. "I don't think that it's a given that if you're pretty, or you have things, you'll be an awful person," I said.

She shrugged. "I suppose not everyone, but that Laura Landers sure couldn't handle it. Like I said, it turned her into an awful, terrible person."

"Why do you say that she was an awful person?" I asked. I needed specifics from her.

"The way she treated Janet and me was terrible. It felt like she didn't even want us in the book club, but the book club was my idea to begin with. I started it three years ago, and people heard about it and just began joining. That was nice in the beginning, but then Laura Landers showed up one day, and for some reason, she thought she ran the place." She shook her head and rolled her eyes. "What on earth would possess a person to join somebody else's book club, and then think that they can run things? I'll never understand that." Her brow furrowed. "Maybe it was both Janet and me who started the book club. Oh, I don't know. It doesn't matter."

"What did she do to try to run the book club?" Lucy asked.

"Well, for starters, we didn't need a president. Have you heard of anything so ridiculous in all your life? Whoever heard of a book club needing a president?" She rolled her eyes again. "It was Janet's book club. She started it and it was running just fine until Laura stepped in. She said that we needed to vote for a president. And, of course, she had brought some of her friends along with her, so who do you think they were going to vote for? They were going to vote for her. And before I knew it, she was controlling everything."

"But I thought you couldn't be president for more than one year? And then you had to take two years off? If the book club was started three years ago, how come she was still president?" Lucy asked.

I nodded. It was an excellent question.

She snorted. "That rule about not being a president for more than one year is something new that we started this year. Because Laura has been president for the last two and a half years. Janet had to insist that we have this rule. Otherwise, she was never going to not be the president. That's why she brought her friends along with her so that she would be assured of getting their votes and running the thing."

"That had to be frustrating," I said. "I wouldn't like it one bit if somebody came in and took over my book club and started making up rules. I wouldn't like it at all." And clearly, Patty did not like it either.

She nodded, leaning forward. "Exactly. But nobody seems to care about how I feel about the situation. I mean, Janet cares, but she hasn't had any more success than I have in regaining control of the book club. I was waiting for December when we would all have another vote for a new president, not that it would have mattered. I could imagine her friend

Adriana getting voted in after her, but eventually, she would run out of friends, wouldn't she?"

I felt a little sorry for Patty. It sounded like all she and Janet had wanted to do was start a book club where they and some others could get together and discuss a book every month, but it seemed Laura had turned it into something else. "I'm sorry you were having trouble with Laura and her friends."

She pressed her lips together, then said, "I appreciate hearing that. And as you can see, it's not a surprise that somebody murdered her. I'm sure there was something else that she took over from somebody else, and they got angry and killed her. Really, she deserved it, and I'm not at all surprised."

"Oh, you can't mean that," I said. "She didn't deserve to be shot. No one deserves to be murdered."

She nodded. "She sure deserved it. And sometimes people get what they deserve. I'm not about to feel sorry for her at all."

I was surprised that Patty was so open about her feelings about Laura's murder. "Patty, you said something to Laura at the book club the other night. What was it?"

She narrowed her eyes at me. "Are you going to tell your husband?"

I shook my head. "No, not if you don't want me

to." That was probably a lie. If it was important to the case, then of course I was going to tell Alec.

She sighed angrily. "I told her she had better shut her mouth, or I was going to shut it for her. She had no business saying those things about Lloyd Walker the way she did. But she just laughed at me. She didn't care about anything I had to say." She crossed her arms in front of herself, her jaw twitching.

I was stunned. Clearly, Alec had not interviewed Patty yet because if he had she would have become a suspect. Or at least I believed she would. "I'm sorry that she wasn't kinder about the book you and Janet had chosen for the book club. Everybody deserves to have some respect for their choice of books."

She settled back against the couch again. "Thank you. I appreciate you saying that. I would never have harmed Laura, but I certainly would have liked to."

Lucy and I glanced at one another.

"Patty, I don't blame you one bit for being angry with Laura. Neither of us do," Lucy assured her.

We stayed and visited with Patty for a few minutes before leaving.

"Wow," Lucy said as we walked down the steps.

"You can say that again. She's going to get herself in trouble if she keeps talking that way."

Although I had said I wouldn't say anything to

Alec, there was no way that I couldn't. Could Patty be Laura's killer? Maybe. But we'd have to do some more investigating to know for sure.

CHAPTER 13

The following morning, I woke with a start. It was still dark out, and Alec was snoring softly beside me. I gave him a shake, and he woke up with a snort and sat up. "What? What's going on? Did the phone ring?"

"No. I just thought of something."

He looked at me, his hair standing up on the side of his head. "What?"

"The morning we discovered Laura's body, Adriana Bartle came running up from the other direction, and she wasn't wearing a hat of any kind."

He gazed at me, his eyes still cloudy with sleep. "So?"

"You found a knit hat beneath one of the benches that line the running trail. Maybe it was her hat. What color was the hair inside of it? There was hair in it, wasn't there?"

He closed his eyes, and his head wobbled a moment before he laid back down on the pillow. "We haven't gotten anything back from the lab yet, and there wasn't any hair that I could see. Why? Do you think it's Adriana's?"

"It makes sense, doesn't it?" I asked, laying back down beside him. "She was running toward us without a hat, and it was cold out. Everyone wears a hat when it's this cold outside, and yet she didn't have one."

"What difference does it make? Not everybody is completely prepared when they go for a run."

I shook my head. "Adriana isn't a newbie. She's been running for some time, and she would know that she needs to wear a hat in that kind of weather. She has to be the killer."

He yawned before answering. "Not everybody wears a hat when they go out running in the cold. And why would she want to kill Laura? I thought they were best friends?"

I nodded. "Yes, they're best friends, but Janet Dixon down at the library said that they were frenemies. Maybe they argued about something. Adriana was lying about Laura coming down here by herself to run early. Her husband didn't mention that he was supposed to go with her, even though Adriana said that he was. Something's not adding up with her story."

He yawned again and stretched. "We'll have to wait until the lab has analyzed the hat and they send it back to us. If it was Adriana's hat, they'd be able to trace any hair or skin cells back to her. But for now, we don't know who the killer is." He turned and looked at the clock on the bedside table and groaned. "I could have slept another forty-five minutes."

"Sorry. I don't know why I didn't put it together earlier, but it just came to me as I was waking up." I sat up. "I'm going to go for a run. Do you want to come?"

He was silent for a moment as he lay there with his eyes closed. Then, as the light filtered through the curtains on the window, he murmured, "Yeah. I've been slacking lately."

I got out of bed and went to get my running clothes. It made sense that Adriana was the killer. The two kept one another around to make sure the other wasn't gossiping about them. Or they were jealous of one another. Or something. And how had Adriana managed to show up where Laura lay dead just after her body was discovered? Something was going on there.

***

Alec went to work after our morning run, and Lucy and I headed over to Main Street Duds to see if Adriana was around. We needed to speak with her again.

Once inside, I spotted Adriana in the back, straightening purses that hung on a wall. I nudged Lucy, and we headed over to that back corner.

"Good morning, Adriana," I said. I picked up a black satchel-style handbag from the hook on the wall. "This is cute."

Adriana turned to us. "Good morning, Allie. Good morning, Lucy. We just got a new shipment of handbags in, and I like that one too."

I held it out to Lucy to inspect.

"This is cute," she said, taking it from me and looking inside. "It has a lot of compartments and zippered pockets. That's exactly what I need."

"I love it." I turned to Adriana. "How are you doing, Adriana? We've been thinking about you, and we decided we needed to stop in and check to see how you are."

She smiled sadly. "I'm taking it one day at a time. I still can't believe Laura is gone. I can't tell you how many times a day I pick up my phone to call her and then realize that she isn't there. It's like losing her all over again multiple times a day." Tears sprang to her eyes, and she blinked them away.

"I'm so sorry," I said. "I know this has to be so incredibly hard for you." If Adriana was truly grieving for her best friend, then my heart went out to her. But if she was the killer, then she deserved to go to jail.

She nodded, choking back tears. "I just don't know how I'm going to get through this. What am I going to do for the rest of my life without my best friend? I don't even know."

"I'm so sorry that you're suffering," Lucy said quietly, and she closed the purse. "I just hope the police can find the killer soon. It won't bring her back, but at least it will give her loved ones closure."

She nodded as she hung a purse up on a hook. "That's the only thing we have now. Closure. It's not much, but it will have to do."

"Adriana, now that you've had more time to think about things, have you remembered anything that might help with the case? Maybe something came to you as you were thinking things over?"

She sighed. "The only thing I can think of is that Patty Jackson had to have killed her. I've been thinking and thinking, and she's the only person who makes sense. I mean, if it wasn't her husband. But as I've thought things over, I don't think her husband would do something like this." She hesitated. "Well, I don't know. I guess he could have. Maybe I'm losing my mind from thinking about this so much." She smiled sadly.

"Why do you think Patty might have done it?" I asked.

She sighed. "That darn book club. Patty acts like it belongs to her. She was resentful of anyone who made suggestions about how to make it a better book club. It sounds so silly, doesn't it? It's just a book club. Patty was always angry at Laura because she felt Laura had taken it over. But Laura and I had always wanted to have a book club, and when we found out there was one at the library, we joined. There were only three other people when we got there, and there was just so much room for improvement. We made suggestions, and the other ladies agreed to it, and more people joined the group. But Patty resented everything."

"It sounds like she's set in her ways," Lucy said.

She nodded. "That's exactly what it is. Patty is bossy, controlling, and completely unyielding when it comes to suggestions on how to do things better." She rolled her eyes. "That woman. I swear, I don't think she gets along with anyone."

"Do you really think she would kill over something like that, though?" I asked. I couldn't imagine it, but I didn't know Patty that well.

She nodded. "You don't know how seriously she takes the book club."

"Does she have a gun?" I asked. This was Maine, and a lot of people hunted, so they had guns. But Laura had most likely been killed with a handgun, and I couldn't imagine Patty being a hunter, anyway.

She nodded. "She has a handgun. I know because she carries it in her purse, and I've seen it twice at the book club. She'll be digging in her purse for something, and there's the gun, right there."

I was surprised anyone would bring a gun to a book club. "I wonder if she carries it everywhere."

She nodded. "I'm sure she does. I pointed it out one day, and she got snippy with me and said it was none of my business, and that if a woman wanted to protect herself, then she had every right to do so."

"I'd hate to cross her in an alley on a dark night," Lucy said. "I have a feeling that she wouldn't hesitate to defend herself."

Adriana nodded. "Exactly. I told Laura that she shouldn't tease her because it might get her into trouble. Laura enjoyed doing that kind of thing, you know. Poking fun at Patty and Janet occasionally. It was nothing serious; it's not like it was bullying or anything, but it was something she did from time to time."

"That doesn't sound like a smart thing to do if she

knew Patty was carrying a gun," I said. I picked up another purse and looked inside, but it only had one small, zippered compartment, and I put it back.

She nodded. "That's what I thought, but you couldn't tell Laura anything. And in that way, she and Patty were a lot alike because they were both stubborn."

I suppose you could say that this all made sense, except for one thing. "How would Patty have known that Laura was on the running trail? Hadn't she gone earlier than usual? And how would Patty have known anything about what she did in her personal life?"

She hesitated, then shook her head. "I guess I don't know the answer to that. Patty knew that we ran most days because we talked about it at the book club, but I don't know how she would have known that Laura had gone earlier that morning. I don't know if we ever discussed what time we went running."

"Did Laura do that often? Go running earlier than normal?" Lucy asked. "I know you said she had a reason for doing it that morning, but was it a common thing for her to change her plans at the last minute?"

She shrugged. "She did it occasionally. Not often, but it wasn't unusual either. Sometimes things come up, and you just can't stick with your original plans."

I nodded. "What time did you start your run that day, Adriana?" I asked.

She looked at me, a hint of surprise in her eyes, but it was gone just as quickly as it had appeared. "I guess I had been running for about half an hour by the time I ran into the two of you. Why?"

I shrugged. "You didn't see anybody else on the trail? We didn't see anyone."

She shook her head. "No, I didn't see anyone. But she was close to Emmons Drive, and the killer could have driven up and parked there at the entrance to the running trail and then taken off after they shot her. They must have had a suppressor, though. I didn't see anybody coming out of those houses."

"Some of them heard the sirens, and they stepped outside or were looking through their windows," I said. "But I guess none of them heard the gunshot."

She nodded knowingly. "Then the killer must have had a suppressor. I don't see how they could have missed it otherwise. I just don't know what could have happened to Derrick. Why wasn't he there with her? If he isn't the killer, then he should have been there to protect her, and yet he wasn't. Did Alec ask him about that?"

I shrugged. "Alec doesn't always tell me the details of everything he finds out, so I don't really know. But I know that he's on top of things and would definitely ask questions like that, so it wouldn't surprise me if he talked to Derrick about it."

She nodded. "Okay then, since he hasn't been arrested, the killer has to be Patty. The more I think about things, the more I think it has to be her. And it wouldn't surprise me if Janet helped her."

"Why?" I asked. Now she was dragging Janet into this, and it made me wonder if she was making things up.

"They're together a lot. I could see one of them driving the car and the other jumping out to shoot her. They would need to get away quickly after they committed the murder. It just makes sense, don't you think?" she asked.

I wasn't sure if it made sense or not, but it was certainly possible. "Maybe."

But I didn't like the scenario. I couldn't see either Patty or Janet being athletic, and the scene that she was describing would mean that the shooter had to have run back to the car and gotten in quickly. It didn't seem possible for either of the elderly ladies.

CHAPTER 14

"I just thought of something."

I turned to look at Lucy. We were headed over to the Cup and Bean to get some coffee. It was early, and I needed a great big cup of coffee to stay awake. "What?"

"Remember when I was reading Lloyd's book to you? There was a note jotted down inside of it."

I had completely forgotten about it. "Yeah, I remember. What about it?"

"I don't know. It just seemed kind of cryptic."

"Do you think the killer left it? Is that what you're saying?"

She was quiet for a moment. Then she shrugged. "I don't know. It would be weird for them to do that, wouldn't it? But still, the note was weird itself."

"Do you remember what it said?" I asked, trying to think back on it.

She shook her head. "No, I don't remember. I just thought it sounded odd when I read it. Maybe we should go to the library and look for that book and reread it. Maybe it's a clue."

I frowned. "How could it be a clue? Laura wasn't even dead at the time."

"I know, but what if they were sending her a message, only she got the wrong book?"

"Okay, now I'm intrigued. What if the killer really was trying to send her a warning, but she never got it? And maybe she did whatever it was they were warning her against because she didn't even know about it?"

She nodded. "What if that's what happened? We need to get to the library and find that book. Oh, I hope it's not checked out."

"Okay, but first we need coffee. Alec was up and out of the house early this morning, so I didn't even bother making a pot."

This could get interesting.

"Okay, coffee first, then to the library."

* * *

The library was empty other than Janet and another librarian sitting back behind the counter. I nodded and gave them a little wave as we hurried back to the bookshelf where we had gotten our book from.

"Oh, no," I said.

"Oh no, what?" Lucy said from behind me. And then she said, "Oh."

I turned to look at her. "Better start looking." Laura hadn't been kidding about Lloyd donating a bunch of copies of his book to the library. Everybody in the book club must have had one by the time we came to get a book. There was only one left then. There were now fifteen books on the shelf. I grabbed the first one and opened it. "Where was the message located? I never looked at it."

"It's on the third page of chapter one." She flipped through a book she had picked up and then closed it and put it back.

"Got it." The book I picked up was also empty of any messages jotted down in pencil, so I put it back and grabbed another. This one wasn't t either, so I closed it and grabbed another.

"Thank goodness it'll be easy to find. It was written in pencil in the margins," she said.

I nodded and grabbed another book. "Nothing here." I closed it and grabbed another.

"Here it is," she said, opening a book. She read it out loud and looked up at me. "What does that sound like? Does it sound like a warning?"

I came over to stand beside her and read it. *"Under the light of the full moon, the truth shall emerge from the shadows, revealing what hides in plain sight."* I thought for a moment. "I don't know for sure. It sounds like it could be a threat. But was it really meant for Laura?"

"Maybe it was just someone working on their poetry."

I nodded. "I guess that's possible, but why would they write it in this book?"

We both stared at the handwriting in pencil for a minute, trying to come up with what it might mean. Before we came up with anything, I heard the front door scrape across the threshold, and then a voice. "I want to speak to the manager!"

Lucy and I looked at each other. "The manager?" I said, making a face.

"Right now! I want to speak to the manager!"

"That sounds like Lloyd Walker," Lucy whispered.

We tiptoed to the end of the aisle and peered around the corner. Sure enough, Lloyd was standing near the doorway, a cane hooked over one arm and wearing a heavy suede jacket unzipped with the collar of his shirt open. He wore a gray tweed hat on his head, and he stood with his arms wide as if he were going to give someone a giant bear hug, but the look on his face said he was not in the hugging mood.

"Lloyd, what's the matter?" Janet asked from behind her desk.

"I demand to speak to the manager!" He took a step and nearly stumbled, but somehow caught himself, then staggered across the floor to the front counter. When he got there, he slammed a fist on the top. "Right now! I need to speak to a manager."

Janet sighed. "Oh, come on Lloyd, you know a library doesn't have a manager. What are you thinking?" She got up from her desk and came around to the counter. "What is it you need?"

I glanced over my shoulder at Lucy and shrugged. She shook her head, and we turned back to watch.

"I demand that this so-called book club that's meeting here be disbanded. You have no right to use my book to defame me," he slurred.

"Lloyd, no one is trying to defame you. Patty and I suggested we read your book because we were sure that everyone would enjoy it as much as Patty and I did. Can we help it if no one else has good taste?" Janet said matter-of-factly.

He shook his head. "That evil woman spread gossip about me around this town. She said that I was a hack and that I had no talent whatsoever. I talked to Bill Evarts down at the bank, and he told me she told him that herself. Said he couldn't see any reason why he should read the book since that woman said it was so bad. Don't you see how that is going to affect my sales?"

"Oh, I'm sorry, Lloyd," Janet said. "If I had had any idea that it would cause you trouble, I never would have suggested that we read your book. But I'm sure that people are going to want to make up their own mind about your book and read it themselves."

We scooted a little closer to the end of the aisle so we could hear better because Janet was speaking in lowered tones.

He shook his head. "It's going to be the ruination of me. I am not a hack. I have been studying writing for decades. Why, my editor said I had the talent to become the next James Patterson."

She reached across the counter and patted his hand. "Oh, I know you do, and it shows in your writing. Don't worry about that woman. She's gone now, and she can't hurt you anymore."

Lucy and I looked at each other and then turned back to what was unfolding in front of us. Were we about to find out who the killer was?

He shook his head. "It serves her right that she was murdered. She was an awful woman. I bet she did this sort of thing to a lot of people, and somebody just got tired of it."

Janet looked over her shoulder at the other librarian, who had been glancing up at the two of them as they spoke. Janet turned back to Lloyd. "I know for a fact that she did that to lots of people. She was always criticizing people and spreading gossip about them around town. She told everybody that Patty had an affair with her next-door neighbor last year, and nothing could be further from the truth. It humiliated Patty, and she confronted her, and Laura laughed about it. So you're right, she's done this sort of thing before, but somebody got tired of her antics, and they put an end to her, so we don't have to worry about her anymore."

Lucy and I gasped and turned to look at each other. "An affair?" I whispered.

"With her neighbor?" she whispered back.

We both turned back to see what else they would say.

Lloyd held onto the counter, swaying, obviously drunk at such an early hour of the morning. "Well, I'm certainly not going to feel sorry for her then. She should have kept her mouth shut, and she would still be alive today. I'd like to shake the hand of the person who pulled the trigger. Would you happen to know who that was, so I can congratulate them?"

I was shocked that this conversation was even happening, but I hoped Janet would know. She shook her head, and I sighed in disappointment. "No, I don't know who it was, but they did this town a favor. Not that I'd like to see anybody murdered, of course, but like you, I cannot feel sorry for her either."

He snorted. "Some people need to learn to shut their mouths."

At that moment, Lucy let the book slip from between her fingers, and it landed on the carpet with a dull thud. If there had been more people in the library, I doubted anybody would have heard it, but as it was empty, both Janet and Lloyd turned and looked in our direction.

His brow furrowed. "What are you doing back there? Are you eavesdropping? Are you? Do you know what happens to people who eavesdrop?"

I shook my head. "No, we were just going to check out a book, and it slipped from my hands." I went to pick it up, giving Lucy a look. She shrugged. "As a matter of fact, this is your book, Lloyd," I said. We hurried to the front counter, and I laid it on top. "Janet, we didn't quite get to finish the book the first time we checked it out, and we wanted to know how everything plays out." I smiled at Lloyd.

He scowled. "I bet you did. You don't have any right to read my book."

"Now, Lloyd," Janet soothed. "It's good that people want to read your book." She winked at me.

"I enjoyed your book," Lucy said. "We're going to finish it up and then return it so somebody else can check it out."

He looked at me. "I heard you were married to that detective who's hunting for that woman's killer. You tell him she deserved to die, and nobody should be punished for it."

I could smell the booze coming off of his breath, and I took a step back. "My husband is going to uphold the law, and when he finds her killer, they will go to jail for a very long time."

He breathed out through his mouth, and the smell of booze nearly gagged me. "Suit yourself, then, but don't be surprised if you can't find the killer. I think they're going to be wily and maintain their freedom. That's what I think." With that, he spun around, almost falling, but caught himself by slipping the cane off his arm and digging it into the floor. After regaining his composure, he stomped out the door.

I turned to Janet. "Well, it's a little early for drinking."

She smiled. "You know how writers are. They like to drink." Lucy and I looked at one another as Janet scanned the book for us.

CHAPTER 15

Lucy looked at me. "What do you suppose that is supposed to mean?"

I read the message aloud and thought for a moment, then shook my head. "I don't know if it's supposed to mean anything at all. But maybe—," I trailed off.

"Maybe what?"

My eyes met hers. "Maybe you were right. Maybe it was a warning, and Laura was supposed to get this book."

"But everyone at the book club checked out a book. How would she have been the one to get this copy?"

I shook my head. "I don't know. Let's grab a coffee and go see Alec. Maybe it will make sense to him."

"A coffee sounds good."

I drove over to the Cup and Bean, and we went through the drive-through and ordered three coffees. I knew Alec would appreciate some caffeinated sustenance. Not to mention a tasty muffin.

I KNOCKED on Alec's office door, and when he hollered to come in, I pushed the door open. He smiled when he saw us.

"Good morning."

I nodded and held up the coffee and the little paper bag with his muffin in it. "Good morning. I've brought gifts."

He chuckled. "That's fantastic. I've already had two cups of the slop they call coffee here at the station, and I am ready for something that tastes good."

I entered the tiny office with Lucy following behind me and set his coffee and muffin on his desk, then leaned over and kissed him. "Then you're in luck. I predict both the coffee and muffin will be tasty." I sat down in the chair in front of the desk, and Lucy sat next to me. She was carrying our coffee and muffins and she put my coffee and muffin on the desk in front of me.

"How's it going, Alec?" she asked. "Anything new? Have you found Laura's killer?"

Alec took a long sip of his coffee, closed his eyes for a moment, and smiled. He opened his eyes. "Not yet, but I'm on their trail. What brings you girls by? Don't tell me you just wanted to do me a favor and bring me coffee and a muffin?" He opened the bag and nodded. "Blueberry. My favorite."

I took a sip of my coffee, a vanilla latte. "Well, as much as we would enjoy coming to visit you, we came about a murder."

He looked at me, eyebrows raised. "Wait, there hasn't been another murder, has there?"

I shook my head. "No, silly. We came about Laura's murder." I reached into my handbag and pulled out the book, opening it to the first chapter. "When we got this book to read for the book club, we saw this message written in it. Of course, at that time, Laura was still alive, so we didn't think much of it. But the more we've been thinking and talking about it, the more we're wondering if maybe it has something to do with her murder."

"Yes, we were wondering if maybe it was a message to Laura, but Laura didn't get it because we got the book with the message in it."

Alec pulled the book toward himself and read the

message. He shook his head. "I don't know. Is it a threat? It sounds like it could be."

I shrugged. "We don't know; we were just wondering if maybe it would make sense to you since you've been investigating the case."

He read it again. "I don't know if it means anything, but it's interesting." He looked up at me. "So you think somebody left a warning for Laura, but somehow the two of you ended up with the book instead of her?"

I shrugged. "It's a possibility. But to be honest, there were about fifteen of these books on the shelf at the library today. The chances of her picking up the right book would have been pretty low." I suddenly felt silly for bringing this over for him to look at. It couldn't mean anything, could it?

He nodded. "Well, I can't see how it relates to the murder since she was still alive when you saw it, but I'll keep it in mind." He took a bite of his muffin and nodded. "The Cup and Bean has good muffins. They don't compare to yours, of course, but they're pretty good."

"I like them, too," I said. I took a bite of my muffin. It was nice sometimes to have somebody else do the baking.

"So how is the case coming, Alec?" Lucy asked. "Do you have anybody in your sights yet? I sure hope that you've got somebody that you're going to arrest soon."

He shook his head. "I wish I had somebody to arrest, too. But so far, all I've got are people I've talked to about the murder."

"So what happened with that knit hat you found on the running trail? Did you find out anything about it?" I asked.

He looked at me for a moment. "We got a report back from the lab. There was a brunette hair that I missed inside the hat, and an analysis was done on it. The hat belongs to Adriana Bartle."

Lucy and I both gasped. "So, she is the killer!" I said. "Why haven't you arrested her?" Lucy and I turned to look at each other.

Lucy nodded at me. "She's the killer. I knew she was one of those phony friends you can't trust."

Alec sat back in his chair. "I haven't arrested her because I don't think she's the killer."

I shook my head. "What are you talking about? Of course, she's the killer. You've got proof. She was there at the scene. She probably circled around and came running up when she knew somebody had discovered the body. All those tears trying to act innocent, but she wasn't. She's the killer."

Alec was quiet for a moment, then he picked up his cup of coffee. "There's a possibility that's what happened, but I don't think so. Mostly because her husband is her alibi. She said she was home until 7:30 AM. That would have given her just enough time to get to the running trail and run as far as where the body was. She wouldn't have had the time to kill Laura and escape. She wasn't wearing clothes that would have concealed the weapon and she would have needed time to get rid of it."

I stared at him, taking this in. "But it was a gunshot. It only took one gunshot to kill Laura. If Adriana is a fast runner, she easily could have circled back around and then come up on us the way she did."

"Maybe she ditched the gun in a bush," Lucy suggested.

He nodded. "I agree. If she was a fast runner, it wouldn't have taken much for her to do that. But we don't have any other evidence linking her to the crime. She said she lost the hat there three days earlier and didn't realize it until she had gotten home. It wasn't important enough for her to go back and retrieve it since it wasn't an expensive hat. She also doesn't own a gun."

"Maybe she got one on the black market," Lucy said, turning to me. "She could have purchased it on the black market so it couldn't be traced back to her, and then she killed Laura and disposed of the gun. It's probably at the bottom of the lake as we speak."

"But how would she have driven to the lake, disposed of the gun, and then circled back around to run up the running trail in the little time she had?" Alec asked.

"She could have hidden it somewhere. A bush like Lucy said, or her car had to be parked somewhere along the running trail, and it could have been in the trunk. When she left, she could have tossed it into a lake," I suggested.

He nodded. "I don't see a woman like Adriana Bartle as knowing anybody who deals with black market items. Do you?"

He had a point. Adriana was not the type of woman who would know any unsavory characters. Even so, her hat was at the crime scene. "Did any of the people who live around there hear anything? An argument? The gun going off?"

"Or a scream from Laura when she knew she was about to be murdered?" Lucy asked.

He shook his head. "Everybody claims they didn't hear a thing. I'm not saying that I am completely ruling Adriana out, but I certainly don't have enough evidence to arrest her yet. I'll keep an eye on her and see how things go."

I groaned. "Something has to give. There has to be

some kind of evidence that we're overlooking, and that will prove who the killer is."

"I agree," Lucy said. "There has to be something somewhere. A woman doesn't get murdered out in the open like that without somebody having seen or heard something."

Alec took a sip of his coffee and sighed. "Many of the residents had already gone to work that morning. But if she had a suppressor on the gun, that would explain why no one heard anything. At that end of the running trail, the houses sit back away from the trail, so it's not surprising that nobody saw anything either."

I sighed. "Back to the drawing board."

It bothered me we didn't know more about Laura's death than we did. We had to dig deeper and come up with answers.

CHAPTER 16

After I dropped Lucy off at her house, I headed over to the grocery store for a much-needed pantry and refrigerator stock-up. Grocery shopping wasn't one of my favorite chores to do, and I had put it off a few days longer than I should have.

My first stop was the produce department. I had been in the mood for an apple pie, so I decided some Granny Smith apples were in order. You can make an apple pie from other apples, but you'll end up with a different flavor. That's not always a bad thing, and I sometimes used different apples for various apple desserts, but nothing beats an apple pie made with Granny Smith apples.

I finished picking out the perfect apples for my pie

and turned to the display of berries. They had blueberries, blackberries, raspberries, and strawberries. I picked up a plastic clamshell box of the most perfect-looking raspberries I'd ever seen. Maybe I would add those to my apple pie, or maybe I would come up with another dessert with just the raspberries. I set them in the front of my shopping cart and glanced around the produce department. Alec loved sweet potatoes, so I headed over to the potato display.

"Hey, Allie," Dennis Crane said. Dennis worked in the produce department and was the friend that Derrick Landers had gone fishing with.

I smiled, hoping this conversation would be fruitful—pardon the pun. "How are you doing, Dennis? The produce is looking fantastic today."

He grinned. "Well, I'm glad to hear it. We do our best to bring in the freshest produce we can."

I nodded as I picked up a small sweet potato and looked it over.

"Dennis, how have things been going? I didn't see you in here the last time I stopped in. You must have been on vacation." I pulled a plastic bag from the roll to put my sweet potatoes in.

He smiled again. "Yeah, I was on vacation. A buddy of mine and I always go fishing for a week when the ice finally melts off the local lakes."

"Oh? Did you rent a cabin? Alec and I have been

talking about taking a vacation and renting one of those cabins out in the woods. I think it would be a lot of fun, but Alec isn't so sure. He's more of an indoor person, other than when he goes running."

"No, we didn't rent a cabin. We probably should have, but we just got up early each morning and got down to the local lakes to fish. There are three of them we like to go to, so we just switched off each day going to a different one."

"Well, you must be an avid fisherman, then." I picked up another sweet potato and kept my eyes on him.

He nodded as he stacked large russet potatoes in the nearby bin. "I love to fish. I swear, I could do it every day of my life. I told my wife that when I retire, she's never going to see me because I'll be down at the lake. I can hardly wait, but I guess I'm going to have to because I've got another 20 years to go before I can retire." He laughed. "Twenty years. Can you believe it? Maybe I'll strike it rich and be able to retire early."

I grinned. "Wouldn't that be fun? Striking it rich and retiring early? I think that's just about everybody's dream. How does your wife feel about your fishing?"

He shrugged. "She likes seafood, so she doesn't argue with me. I can usually bring home a few fish each time I go, and right now our freezer is on its way to being fully stocked with whatever is biting."

"Oh, lucky you," I said. "I've got to buy my fish here at the grocery store. I bet it tastes a lot better when you catch it yourself."

He put some more potatoes into the bin. "You bet it does. It's always better when you catch it yourself."

"You said you went with a buddy. Who did you go with?"

He looked up at me. "Derrick Landers. We've been friends for years."

"Oh, goodness," I said, hesitating with another sweet potato in my hand. "Wasn't he married to Laura Landers?"

He nodded, growing somber. "Yes, he was married to Laura. I still can't get over the fact that she was murdered like she was."

I shook my head sadly. "It's such a terrible shock, isn't it? Just between the two of us, my friend Lucy and I were running on the running trail that morning, and we discovered her body."

His eyes went wide. "Oh no. That had to have been terrible. I'm so sorry that you two were the ones who found her. It must have been awful."

I sighed. "It really was. We're still in shock that it was her. I can't imagine who would have wanted to kill her like that. Can you?"

He gazed at me for what felt like a moment too long, and then he shook his head. "No, I can't imagine who would want to do such a thing. She was always such a sweet person. I got to know her fairly well since Derrick and I are such good friends. She always teased him about bringing home all that fish. She never cared much for it, but Derrick loves it, so she cooked it for him."

I nodded. "I knew Laura, and you're right—she was always so sweet. Happy and bubbly every time I ran into her. I don't suppose Derrick has any idea who might have wanted to kill her?"

He shook his head. "No. I think he was so completely blindsided by this that he's still in shock. Isn't your husband working on the case?"

I nodded, leaning on my shopping cart. "Yes, he's working on the case, but he doesn't always give me the details of cases like this. There are things he likes to keep to himself until he has more information, so I don't know what Derrick said to him."

He put both hands on the plexiglass barrier that kept the potatoes from rolling onto the floor. "Well, I know Derrick is completely broken up over this, and no one can blame him." He gazed at me again. "But there's something that I've been thinking about. Between the two of us, when your husband Alec showed up where we were fishing that morning,

Derrick said we had been fishing since earlier in the morning. But that wasn't quite true."

I stepped in closer. "What do you mean?"

He took a deep breath before answering. "We had only been there for about twenty minutes. We had just barely gotten our lines into the water. At the time, I thought he was just confused because Alec had just told him that his wife was dead. Honestly, I was so in shock that I didn't think about what he was saying. I was still trying to take in the fact that Laura had been murdered. But I've thought about it since then, and it really wasn't true, you know. I don't know if Derrick has corrected that with Alec. I'm sure he's talked to him a few times since her death."

I hesitated before answering and then nodded. "Yes, I'm sure that Alec has talked to him several times. Both to keep him apprised of the investigation and also to verify facts about what happened that morning." For Dennis to be bringing this up, it had to bothering him.

He nodded and turned to the cart with the box of potatoes on it, picked up two more, and set them on the display. "I don't know how to bring it up with Derrick. I doubt he even realizes what he said. And probably by this time, Alec already knows that we hadn't been out there fishing for long."

"Was it later than when you normally would have

been out there?" I asked. Fishermen liked to get out to the lake very early, but from his description, they probably had only gotten out there at around 7:00 AM.

He nodded without looking at me. "Yeah, we usually try to get there around five or six o'clock in the morning, so we were a couple hours or so behind. I had been waiting at my house for Derrick to show up and was just about to call him when he honked his horn out front. I grabbed my fishing stuff and went out there, and when I asked where he had been, he just shrugged and said he slept in. I gave him a hard time about it, but then we went on our way and got to the lake and started fishing." He looked up at me and shrugged again. "Stuff happens, you know. Derrick is a good guy, and he loved his wife. I've never had a better friend."

I nodded and stuck another sweet potato into the plastic bag I was holding, then tied the top into a knot and set it in my shopping cart. "Good friends are hard to come by. My friend Lucy and I have been close ever since we met, and I've never had a better friend, so I know what you're talking about."

He smiled, looking slightly guilty now. "Yeah, good friends are hard to find, and when you find one, you need to hold on to them with all your might." He nodded. "Well, I better get back to work. This produce isn't going to put itself on the displays." He chuckled.

I smiled. "No, it's not. You have a good day, Dennis."

"You too, Allie."

I pushed my cart out of the produce department, wondering about what Dennis had told me. Was he worried about it? Did he think Derrick might have had something to do with Laura's death? And had Derrick informed Alec that he was wrong about the time that he had told him they began fishing?

CHAPTER 17

Finding out that Derrick Landers hadn't told Alec the complete truth the morning of Laura's death was surprising. Maybe he had been in shock and wasn't thinking straight. I didn't know if that put him back on our list of suspects or not.

Lucy and I went for our morning run and then stopped by the Cup and Bean for another cup of coffee and a check-in with Mr. Winters. I had been intending to stop by for the past several days, but something had always come up. We ordered our coffees and sat at his table.

He looked up at us from his newspaper and smiled. "Well, if it isn't two strangers, finally stopping by to say hello. You would think that we didn't even know one another."

I sighed. "Oh, Mr. Winters, you know we could never forget you. How have you been? And how is Sadie?" I reached underneath the table and scratched the little poodle's ear.

He grinned and took a sip of his black coffee, setting the cup back down. "Great. I'm doing just great. Well, to tell you the truth, my lumbago is acting up. It's all that rain and cold weather. Spring cold weather differs from winter cold weather, you know? It's wetter, and it has a different effect on my joints."

"My husband says the same thing," Lucy said, taking a sip of her coffee. "He doesn't like the spring at all."

"Thankfully, summer will be here before we know it," I said. "Mr. Winters, did you find out anything about Laura Landry's death? You've had plenty of time to check around."

He narrowed his eyes at me. "I didn't realize I was on the payroll."

I chuckled. "No, you're not on the payroll, and neither are we, and yet we still find time to ask around to try to figure out a murder. Now then, what did you find out?" Mr. Winters could pretend that he had no interest in the case, but I knew better. He might have been an elderly man, but he loved a good juicy gossip session.

He beamed at me. "Okay, fine. I didn't know Laura Landry well at all, but occasionally I ran into her here or around town, and she was always smiling and polite. But as I asked around town, it seemed that some people had a different take on her."

Lucy leaned forward. "What do you mean? What kind of different take?"

He folded his newspaper over and placed it beneath his arms on the table. "Some people were just fine with how she treated them. She was nice and sweet to them. But as I asked around, I discovered some people didn't like her at all. They said she was a backstabber, a liar, and a gossip. Nobody likes a gossip." One eyebrow shot up. "But some had the audacity to say they were glad she was dead."

Lucy feigned a gasp. "They actually said they were glad she was dead? I mean, I get it. Sometimes people don't like one another, but I would never wish for somebody to be dead. Especially not murdered."

He nodded and took another sip of his coffee before continuing, "Apparently, she wasn't as nice as she would have had people believe. Lots of people had something against her, but nobody seemed to know who might have murdered her."

I reached under the table and scratched Sadie's ear

again, taking this in. "I hate to say it, but as we've talked to different people, we've heard the same thing. Some people thought she was the best person ever, and then some didn't like her at all." I was thinking about Janet and Patty. Neither of the two ladies liked her. And Lloyd. We couldn't forget Lloyd.

He nodded. "Sometimes, people portray themselves in a way that they prefer to be seen and not as they actually are. Not that that should surprise anyone."

"It's odd that nobody seems to have any idea who might have wanted to kill her, though," I said absently. "I mean, somebody's got to have an idea, don't they?"

Lucy nodded. "Oh, you can bet that somebody knows something. I think we just haven't run into that person."

Lucy had a point. Maybe we just hadn't talked to enough people.

"What about you two? What have you found out?" he asked.

I shook my head. "Not nearly enough. Alec found a knit hat there at the running trail, but it belonged to a friend of hers, and that friend has an alibi."

He took another sip of his coffee, thinking this over. "How solid is the alibi? Maybe they struggled, and the hat was ripped off of her head, and in her hurry to get away, she didn't pick it up."

I stared at Mr. Winters. Of course that could have happened. What was I thinking? But Alec said that he didn't have enough evidence to arrest Adriana. I nodded. "I think that could have happened. Not that it did, of course, but it could have."

Lucy leaned forward. "Nobody seemed to hear anything that morning, though. If they had been fighting, wouldn't one of them have screamed? I know I would have if I thought I was about to lose my life."

"She may not have seen it coming, though," Mr. Winters pointed out. "Unless the killer was waving the gun around, Laura may not have had any idea she was about to die."

I sighed. "True."

"Allie found out yesterday that Derrick Landers' alibi may not hold up," Lucy blurted out.

I glanced at Lucy. I didn't want that information to get out, but there it was. Alec had been interested in hearing about it and was going to talk to Derrick again.

Mr. Winters looked at me, both eyebrows raised. "Really? So maybe it was the husband. But why would he kill her out there on the running trail? He could have done it in the comfort of his own home. Doesn't make any sense."

"If they were both out there running, maybe they had an argument, and he shot her," I said. Maybe that was really what had happened. Except, why would he have a gun on him when he went running unless he intended to do it.

The door to the coffee shop opened, and Adriana Bartle walked through it. She strode up to the front counter, a look of anger on her face. I nudged Lucy and nodded in her direction.

"Oh," Lucy said under her breath.

Adriana leaned forward and gave the barista her coffee order, and then she glanced around the room. With her eyes on mine, she smiled and gave me a nod. I nodded back, and she turned back to the barista. I wasn't sure what was going on with her, but she seemed upset about something.

When she had gotten her coffee order, she strode over to our table. "Ladies, Mr. Winters," she said with a nod. "How are you this morning? What's new?"

I suddenly felt like she knew we had been talking about her, but I wasn't going to let on. I smiled. "Oh, not much of anything, Adriana. We've just been talking about the weather and hoping for more sunshine."

She narrowed her eyes at me. "Really? That's what you were talking about?"

I nodded. "Yes. How about you, Adriana? How are you doing? I've been thinking about you."

She glared at me. "Well, next time you think about me, you tell your husband to keep his nose out of my business."

I was taken aback by this. "What are you talking about?"

She shook her head and gritted her teeth. "Like you don't know? Don't act innocent with me. He's been talking to my neighbors and my boss. I did not kill Laura. She was my best friend, and there was no way I would ever kill her. I do not appreciate the police sticking their nose in my business and making people suspicious of me. And I also do not appreciate the three of you getting together to sit and gossip about me. I am innocent. You tell your husband that."

I stared at her as she spun around and almost jogged to the door, slamming into it when she got to it. Without looking behind her, she pulled it open and left the coffee shop.

I glanced at Lucy and then at Mr. Winters. "Wow."

"Wow is right," Lucy said. "So Alec must think she's the killer; otherwise, he wouldn't be on her case like that."

I nodded. "I didn't realize he felt so strongly about

her as the killer, especially after he told us she had an alibi. Something must have fallen through." I had told Alec about Derrick's faulty alibi, and he said he would speak to him again, but he had never mentioned that he was going to look more closely at Adriana.

"That was one angry woman," Mr. Winters said. "Alec had better be sure that she's the killer, or that woman is going to take her anger and frustration out on him."

I nodded. "I don't doubt that for a minute."

CHAPTER 18

The following morning, the sun was up and shining brightly. It was another lovely spring day, but the weatherman had said this would be the last of it for at least a week, as we were expecting rainstorms.

"I wish our weather was like this every day," Lucy said. "Even though it's still cold, the sun is just gorgeous."

I nodded as we ran along the street in a neighborhood of modest brick homes. "Me too. I'm all set for lots of sunshine."

We ran along in silence for a few minutes, just soaking up the sun. The neighborhood we ran through had once been a family neighborhood, but as the years went on, the kids had grown and left, and the neighborhood was quiet these days. I glanced ahead and saw a woman working on the brick planters in front of her home. She was dressed in a heavy coat and wore a knit hat and gloves. It was Patty Jackson, and this was no random neighborhood we were running through.

"Target spotted," I said, lowering my voice.

Lucy looked at her. "Right on time."

I nodded. When we got to Patty's house, we slowed down. "Good morning, Patty!" I called.

She looked over her shoulder at me and nodded, slowly standing up straight as if the movement were painful. "Morning, ladies." She limped slightly as she approached us. "What are you doing out here at this time of day?"

I smiled. We were wearing our running leggings, and it should have been obvious. "Just going for our morning run. We rarely run in this neighborhood, but we wanted a change of scenery." I chuckled lightly.

She nodded. "I guess that's why I haven't seen you run through here before. Mighty cold weather for running around like that."

"The exercise keeps us warm," I said.

"What are you up to, Patty?" Lucy asked.

She gestured with her thumb back toward her planter. "Got to get everything weeded and ready for new flowers. I'm tired of this cold weather, and my joints can't stand it, but I want fresh flowers growing in my planters, so I've got to get out and get it done."

"I love fresh flowers growing in front of the house," I said. "It gives a house such a homey feel."

She nodded. "I agree. I've never not had flowers growing in my planters, and this will not be the year that I don't have them." She laughed. "That's a complicated way of saying I'm going to have my flowers."

"I've got to get my planters done too," Lucy said. "I hate doing the weeding, though. We're supposed to have rain this coming week; maybe after the soil gets loosened up from all that rain, I'll get to work on mine."

She nodded. "I'm hoping it's the last heavy rain that we'll get for a while."

"Patty, how have you been?" I asked.

She shrugged. "Other than my joints aching, I've been just fine. Has your husband found Laura Landers' murderer yet?"

I tilted my head so the sun wasn't shining directly in my eyes. "Not yet, but he's working diligently to find them. I still can't get over the fact that Laura was murdered, and I can't imagine who would want her dead."

She made a clicking sound and shook her head. "Well, I can't imagine who actually murdered her, but

I think there are plenty of people in this town who wouldn't mind her being dead."

I wasn't surprised to hear her say it, but I still didn't understand the thought that it would be good for somebody to be dead. "Patty, you can't mean that. I know some people are unkind and just downright obnoxious, but dead? Murder? I just don't understand that."

She shrugged. "Maybe it sounds harsh, but that would have been the only way that woman would have kept her mouth shut and left people alone."

"Was she really that awful?" Lucy asked. "Personally, I never had an issue with her."

She nodded and spit on the ground. "It depended on who you were. She liked to keep up appearances. But some people just didn't matter, and she didn't care how we saw her. Every time I suggested a book at the book club, she looked down on me like I was nothing. Said she wouldn't be caught dead reading some of the books that I suggested."

"Why did you continue going to the book club, then?" I asked.

She shrugged. "It was technically Janet's book club, and we've been friends for years. I felt like quitting the book club would be quitting on her, and I couldn't do that."

"I guess I can understand that," I said.

"But that wasn't all." Her cheeks turned pink.

"Oh?" I said.

She shook her head, looking away. "She told people I was having an affair with my neighbor. Nothing could be further from the truth, and now his wife doesn't trust me." She looked at us with tears in her eyes. "We've been neighbors and friends for twenty years and she won't speak to me."

"I'm so sorry," I said.

Lucy shook her head. "That's awful. Why would she do that?"

"I don't know. She just didn't like me, and she didn't care that I knew it every time we had a book club meeting. One time she saw me having a conversation at the grocery store with Bill, my neighbor, and that's all it took. Speaking of the book club," she said changing the subject, and shoving her hands in her coat pockets. "Janet said we're going to have a special meeting tonight. Are you going?"

I shook my head. "We hadn't heard there was a special meeting of the book club. It's tonight?"

She nodded. "Seven o'clock, just like always. I guess Janet's got some news to tell us."

"What kind of news?" Lucy asked.

She shrugged. "I don't know exactly. But I guess it's news about how we're going to move forward with the book club. I'm kind of looking forward to it without Laura being there. Maybe I'll suggest some books that we can actually enjoy reading."

"Books are important to you, aren't they, Patty?" I asked.

She nodded. "Of course they are. They're all I've got now that my Sid has passed away. Books and my two cats."

I felt sorry for Patty. If that was all she had left in her life, I could see why the book club had been important to her. Laura had made that one bright spot in her life difficult for her, so who was I to judge that she was so angry at Laura or that she was glad she was gone?

"Should we bring something to eat tonight?" Lucy asked. "We haven't had time to finish the new book that we were going to discuss at the meeting next month."

She shrugged. "Food is always good. I like it, and so does everybody else. You should probably make something, Allie."

The way she said it sounded as if she didn't want Lucy to make anything, and Lucy narrowed her eyes at her.

"I think I can whip something up," I said.

She nodded. "Well, I expect I'd better get back to work on my planter. I'll see you ladies tonight." She turned around and hobbled back to the brick planter in front of her house.

"It was good talking to you, Patty. We'll see you tonight," I said, and we started running again.

When we were out of earshot, Lucy looked at me. "Well, Allie, you've got some baking to do."

I chuckled. "I might need some help from you."

"Oh, I don't know about that. It might not be approved of."

I chuckled again. "I can't believe Laura was so awful to Patty."

She shook her head. "Me either. What on earth got into her to do something like that?"

I wondered what Janet had to tell us about the book club. Certainly, if everyone was going to be there, she would behave herself and not say how glad she was that Laura had died, would she? I certainly hoped so.

CHAPTER 19

*L*ucy and I showed up at the library a few minutes early and slipped in the door before Janet had the chance to lock it to the public.

"Good evening, Janet," I said. "Patty told us there was a meeting of the book club, and I made coconut cupcakes."

Janet looked up from where she sat at her desk and smiled. "That's wonderful, Allie. I'm so glad that you made them, but you didn't have to. This is going to be a brief meeting just to discuss the book club and where we're headed with it."

I shrugged. "It's all right. I enjoy baking, and we can all have a cupcake. We'll go back and make some coffee."

Lucy and I headed to the meeting room, and I set the cupcakes on a table while Lucy got working on making a pot of coffee.

"What do you suppose she has in mind?" Lucy said, lowering her voice.

I shook my head. "I don't know, but I'm glad I made a lot of cupcakes if no one else is going to bring anything to eat."

She chuckled. "Patty wanted you to make something."

I grinned. "It's fine. You know I enjoy baking."

A few minutes later, people began streaming into the room until everybody who was expected had arrived. Even Adriana had shown up. She sat at a table by herself, dabbing at her eyes with a tissue now and then. She took a moment out of her dabbing to glare at me, and I smiled back. I don't know why she was so angry at me. Alec had said he had simply asked around about the murder, and her name had come up with several people. He guessed they had jumped to conclusions, thinking he was specifically asking about her and had her in mind as the killer. He didn't, but I wondered if she was making more of it because she felt guilty about something.

Janet hurried over to a small makeshift podium that sat on a table. She was grinning. "I'm so glad that you all made it. As you know, we have lost our book club president, so I thought we needed to make plans on how to move forward. Since I started the book club, I have now stepped in as president. And as president, I'm going to abolish the role of president." She laughed.

There were some hushed gasps from around the room. Lucy and I glanced at one another. Janet was wasting no time stepping in and making changes.

"I enjoy having a president," Jordan Peevy said.

Janet sighed. "Well, when I started this book club, I never intended that there would be a president. That was Laura's idea. And now that she's gone, we are going to do away with that idea. Don't worry, though, I fully expect to ask everyone's opinion about the books that we should read. I would like to have a larger variety of books and not just read trashy romance novels."

"Right, like that last book we read? That was a snooze fest," Adriana said. "I can't imagine why anybody would choose to read a book that boring."

Janet grimaced. "You might think it was boring, but I know that plenty of people have enjoyed Lloyd Walker's books."

"And you don't have to like every book that you read," Patty said. "We all have different opinions on the types of books that we like to read."

"Well, I guess the same could be said for the two of

you, then," Jackie Cranmer said. "You don't like the ones that Laura picked out, and that's enough to make you make these big changes to the group."

"As I said, we will be open to suggestions," Janet said, still smiling. "If anyone has suggestions now, I would be glad to hear them." She glanced around the room as everyone sat and stared back at her.

"Isn't anyone going to say anything about Laura being killed?" Adriana suddenly said. "She was my best friend for over thirty years, and she made a great book club president. Are we not going to talk about her?"

"I'll miss Laura," Jackie said sadly. "I'm so sorry that you lost your best friend."

Adriana sniffed. "Thank you."

"I'll miss her, too," Anna Binkley said. "It's just not fair that this happened to her. I can't imagine who would want to harm her."

"Well, you know how it is. Someday, the truth shall emerge from the shadows, revealing what hides in plain sight," Janet said, chuckling.

Lucy and I looked at each other and then we turned back to Janet. "What did you say, Janet?" I asked.

She smiled. "Someday the truth shall emerge from the shadows, revealing what hides in plain sight. I heard it on a mystery show years ago and it has stuck with me."

Lucy and I looked at each other again. Lucy leaned over toward me. "Did she just say what I think she said?"

I nodded. "I think she did."

"We'll dismiss for tonight," Janet said. "Remember to read your books, and we'll meet up again in two weeks to discuss it."

Lucy and I glanced at one another and we got up and got a cupcake and a cup of coffee. Some of the ladies took cupcakes to go and filtered out of the room. When just Patty and Janet were left, we cleaned up the table that the cupcakes and coffee were on. I glanced at Janet. "You're really glad that Laura's gone, aren't you, Janet?"

She nodded. "I certainly am. With her death went a lot of my problems."

I took a deep breath. "What kind of problems? Just because she was unkind? Those kinds of problems?"

Janet shrugged. "She was hateful toward Lloyd, you know. He didn't deserve to have her say such vile things about his book. She was kind in the book club meeting compared to the way that she spoke about the book outside of the book club. She was horrible."

Patty nodded. "She certainly was. I can't imagine anybody being as mean and awful as she was."

"Well, I can't imagine anybody killing somebody over a book," I said, glancing at Lucy.

"Yes, I feel the same way," Lucy said.

Janet looked up at me. "Are you taking Laura's side? Because it sounds like you're taking her side."

I shrugged. "What if I was?"

She crumpled the paper towel in her hand. "Anyone who takes that woman's side is no better than she was."

I wondered if this was a veiled threat of some kind. "I'm not taking anybody's side; it's just that Laura didn't deserve to die, even if she was mean."

She laughed. "Listen to you. You never had problems with Laura, and you didn't have to deal with her nastiness. Of course you don't think she deserved to die."

"Janet, did you kill Laura?" I asked.

She narrowed her eyes at me. "Why would you ask me something like that? Are you out of your mind? I have never killed anybody in my life."

Patty stared at us, wide-eyed. "What makes you think she would kill her?"

"Why, I don't even own a gun," Janet said. "How on earth would I have shot her?"

Patty's head slowly swiveled around to look at Janet.

"I'm just asking you a question, Janet. Did you kill Laura?" I asked again.

She laughed again. "You've lost your mind, Allie. Now let's get this room cleaned up and go on home."

"Why don't you answer her?" Lucy asked.

Janet waved a dismissive hand at her. "I am just worn out today. I shelved more books than I have ever shelved in my life, I think." She laughed. "As soon as we get out of here, I'm going to go home, take a shower, and get to bed early."

"Why don't you answer her, Janet?" Patty asked.

Janet turned to look at her. "What?"

"Why don't you answer her? Did you kill Laura?" she asked.

"Patty, why would you ask such a thing?" Janet asked, looking surprised.

Patty blinked. "Because you borrowed my gun two days before Laura was murdered."

Lucy and I gasped. "Where is your gun now?" I asked Patty.

She looked at me. "It's in my purse. She gave it back."

At that, Janet lunged for the handbag on Patty's arm, and without thinking, I lunged at Janet.

CHAPTER 20

"Cupcake?" I held the box out to Alec as he stretched in front of the fire.

"Don't mind if I do," he said and took one from the box. "Those were some fancy moves on your part."

I nodded. "I did what I had to do." I took a cupcake for myself and set the box on the coffee table. Wrestling Patty's purse out of Janet's hands had been harder than I would have imagined. For an older gal, Janet was strong. "Did she confess?"

He nodded. "Yes, it took a little pressure, but she confessed. She hated Laura, and the resentment built up over the past couple of years. Her saying hateful things about Lloyd Walker's book was the final straw."

"Why was Lloyd Walker's book important to her?"

"Seems she may have had a crush on him." He took a bite of his cupcake.

I shook my head. "I swear, why don't people just leave the book club instead of murdering people?" I took a bite of my cupcake. It was moist and full of flavor, just the way I liked it.

He chuckled. "Certainly would have made things easier. Easier for all of us."

"I can't believe that she borrowed Patty's gun to kill Laura. If that was ever traced back to Patty, then Patty would have ended up in jail."

Patty told us that Janet had borrowed her gun under the guise of wanting to take it to the shooting range and try it out before she bought a gun of her own for protection. If you asked me, I thought she borrowed it not just to kill Laura but to be able to blame the murder on Patty if anyone ever got wise to the fact that it was the gun used in the murder.

He nodded. "She figured no one would blame a couple of little old ladies for murder."

I turned to him. "What about the note that was written in the book?"

He took a bite of his cupcake before answering. "She wanted to scare Laura with it, but somehow the books got mixed up, and Laura never received the book with the message. It was the last one that was left on the bookshelf, and of course, you and Lucy got it."

I snorted. "I doubt it would have been enough to scare Laura off. I got the impression that Laura was quite satisfied with herself and was happy being the book club president. Idle threats from an anonymous source wouldn't have bothered her."

He nodded. "Janet was surprised that the threat of exposing her as a gossip and an awful person didn't bother her. But then I told her that Laura most likely never saw her message because you and Lucy got the book. She turned pale."

"Because she had hoped that was as far as she would have to take it? Just threatening her?"

"Yup. She became enraged when Laura made no move to leave the book club and didn't even try to be nicer to her. When she found out that Laura was spreading lies about Patty having an affair with her neighbor she said she felt she had no other options. She couldn't let her continue doing that sort of thing."

I sighed. "That's kind of sweet of her to defend her friend that way."

He chuckled. "By murdering the woman causing the problem?"

I shrugged. "She could have found another method to stop her. The murder was uncalled for."

"I'll say."

I turned to look at him. "How did she know where she could find her?"

"She knew Laura was an early morning runner, so she went out to the trail for several days until Laura turned up alone," he said, taking another bite of his cupcake. "And yes, she bought a suppressor for the gun."

"Well, she can't say it was self-defense then." I took a sip of my cocoa as Dixie jumped up on the ottoman and curled up around my feet.

"Maybe you could be the new president of the book club?" he said after we had finished our cupcakes.

I shot him a look. "What? Why would I want to do that?"

He shrugged. "The last two presidents lost their jobs. They need somebody in there who can pick out more exciting books."

I chuckled. "I don't think it's going to be me. Lucy and I have had enough of the book club to last us for a while."

He nodded. "Me too. And I never even attended a meeting."

I shook my head and then laid it on his shoulder. It was the middle of the night, and I was exhausted. It was a shame that Janet couldn't come up with a better way of dealing with her problems. Because even though she and Patty and a lot of people around town didn't like Laura, there were plenty of people who did, and they had lost someone important to them. But I was glad that the killer was in jail now.

The End

Sign up to receive my newsletter for updates on new releases and sales:
https://www.subscribepage.com/kathleen-suzette
Follow me on Facebook:
https://www.facebook.com/Kathleen-Suzette-Kate-Bell-authors-759206390932120

BOOKS BY KATHLEEN SUZETTE:

A PUMPKIN HOLLOW CANDY
STORE MYSTERY

Treats, Tricks, and Trespassing
Gumdrops, Ghosts, and Graveyards
Confections, Clues, and Chocolate

A FRESHLY BAKED COZY MYSTERY SERIES

Apple Pie a la Murder
Trick or Treat and Murder
Thankfully Dead
Candy Cane Killer
Ice Cold Murder
Love is Murder
Strawberry Surprise Killer
Plum Dead
Red, White, and Blue Murder
Mummy Pie Murder
Wedding Bell Blunders
In a Jam
Tarts and Terror
Fall for Murder
Web of Deceit

A FRESHLY BAKED COZY MYSTERY SERIES

Silenced Santa
New Year, New Murder
Murder Supreme
Peach of a Murder
Sweet Tea and Terror
Die for Pie
Gnome for Halloween
Christmas Cake Caper
Valentine Villainy
Cupcakes and Beaches
Cinnamon Roll Secrets
Pumpkin Pie Peril
Dipped in Murder
A Pinch of Homicide
Layered Lies

A COOKIE'S CREAMERY MYSTERY

Ice Cream, You Scream
Murder with a Cherry on top
Murderous 4th of July
Murder at the Shore
Merry Murder
A Scoop of Trouble
Lethal Lemon Sherbet

A LEMON CREEK MYSTERY

Murder at the Ranch
The Art of Murder
Body on the Boat

A Pumpkin Hollow Mystery Series

Candy Coated Murder
Murderously Sweet
Chocolate Covered Murder
Death and Sweets
Sugared Demise
Confectionately Dead
Hard Candy and a Killer
Candy Kisses and a Killer
Terminal Taffy

Fudgy Fatality
Truffled Murder
Caramel Murder
Peppermint Fudge Killer
Chocolate Heart Killer
Strawberry Creams and Death
Pumpkin Spice Lies
Sweetly Dead
Deadly Valentine
Death and a Peppermint Patty
Sugar, Spice, and Murder
Candy Crushed
Trick or Treat
Frightfully Dead
Candied Murder
Christmas Calamity

A RAINEY DAYE COZY MYSTERY SERIES

Clam Chowder and a Murder
A Short Stack and a Murder
Cherry Pie and a Murder
Barbecue and a Murder
Birthday Cake and a Murder
Hot Cider and a Murder
Roast Turkey and a Murder
Gingerbread and a Murder
Fish Fry and a Murder
Cupcakes and a Murder
Lemon Pie and a Murder
Pasta and a Murder
Chocolate Cake and a Murder
Pumpkin Spice Donuts and a Murder

A RAINEY DAYE COZY MYSTERY SERIES

Christmas Cookies and a Murder
Lollipops and a Murder
Picnic and a Murder
Wedding Cake and a Murder

Made in the USA
Coppell, TX
20 June 2025